MW01710458

Tales of The Peshtigo Putzer

As told
by
jerry kiesow

PublishAmerica
Baltimore

At the specific preference of the author, PublishAmerica allowed this work to remain exactly as the author intended, verbatim, without PublishAmerica's editorial input.

First printing

Photos and sketches by jerry kiesow.
Edited by Gina Taucher, Diane Kiesow, Chris Vollmer, and Al Martin.
Master Putzer sketch by Lynne Bergschultz.
Design by jerry kiesow, Lynne Bergschultz, and PublishAmerica.

ISBN: 1-4241-4872-3
PUBLISHED BY PUBLISHAMERICA, LLLP
www.publishamerica.com
Baltimore

Printed in the United States of America

Stories of how one outdoor enthusiast,
his family and friends,
enjoy the four seasons.

Contents

Dedication

This book is dedicated to all who know the true meaning of putzing. To some, this is a terribly disorganized way to go through life, and yet... we putzers do accomplish much and have an awful lot of fun in the process. Of course, none of us are as accomplished as the sage, Mr. P himself.

j.k.

Foreword

"Until we meet in, on, or near the river."

You readers will become quite familiar with that phrase as you peruse the coming pages and read the tales of a man and his outdoor adventures in Peshtigo River Country. And while the chances of any of you actually meeting Mr. Putzer in, on, or near the river are quite slim, those words hold another significance—they take you to the place. Even if you are not reading this from the local area, or don't regularly visit Peshtigo Country, never have, or never will, the following tales will make you feel as if you are there, and as if you belong there, enjoying all that the outdoors has to offer.

Putzer doesn't catch many fish, he doesn't kill much game, he's not up on the latest gadgets and gizmos designed more to empty your wallet than fill your freezer. Instead, he's out to enjoy life and all that the great outdoors can add to that total experience. And he's out to share that total experience. Don't spend too much time at any one thing; don't be so serious about one pursuit that you overlook the benefits and enjoyments of another.

So, whether it's canoeing or flyfishing or grouse hunting or sightseeing or philosophizing or even making a trip to the local dump, and whether he's alone, or with Mrs. P, or friends, or grandkids, the lesson is always the same—the outdoors is a great place to putz. It's a healthy place to putz, with the sights, sounds, smells, experiences and company taking your mind off your day-to-day stressors, regardless of what you do while you are there. And even if you can't be there to experience the outdoors or Putzer's activities firsthand, his words will make you feel as if you are. And that's a good thing.

So sit back now and enjoy Putzer's antics, learn from his lessons, think about his philosophies, taste his Manhattans, but most of all enjoy the time you have, whether you're in, on, or near his river, or any place else.

Al Martin

Author's note: Without Al, there would be no Peshtigo Putzer. Al gave me the opportunity to bring P to life, for which I am eternally thankful.

j. k.

Prologue

This is not your average outdoor book. Normally, outdoor books are limited to hunting and/or fishing stories. The Putzers enjoy the outdoors in many more ways than hunting and fishing. They bike, they canoe, they ski. They go birding. They can even bring the outdoors into their life when baking Christmas cookies or when purchasing a new hat.

But yes, you will find that they do hunt and fish also.

This is really two books within one. Book I, entitled "In Wishigan Country" has 24 chapters. These tales take place at the Putzers' three season cottage in Marinette County, Wisconsin. That is, unless the cottage is closed, then "Wishigan" moves to Putzer's basement.

Some of these stories have been published before, but not all. Some adventures have been saved just for this book. All of the previously-published stories have been "tweaked," which means they have been updated to reflect present day situations, and corrected to improve the writer's original flaws.

The second book, "Beyond Wishigan," contains new Putzer tales. These take place mostly in Wisconsin, but in a variety of locations and situations in our state. These stories prove that a good putzer can ply his "trade" anywhere.

How did our main character, Mr. P, become the Peshtigo Putzer? This is explained in "The Conception." A tale all its own.

I hope you enjoy this collection as much as I enjoyed putting it together for you.

j.k.

The Conception

This is an introduction to the man you will get to know better as you read each page of this book. Here you get some background, and learn just how he became known as "The Peshtigo Putzer."

Along about thirty, forty years ago, he was invited to an evening out with a business acquaintance—to join in a meeting with *"The Waders of the Wolf."* The *WW* was an intimate and select group of fly fishers who practiced and pursued their passion for trout, naturally, on the Wolf River.

When it came time to introduce himself and tell a bit about his trout fishing life, he had to confess that he had never fished the famed river, but that most of his efforts were concentrated on the Peshtigo. He was, in his own mind, considered an average fisherman who knew just enough about trout and wading to get into trouble. He wanted them to consider him in a way that they could grasp, so he dubbed himself, "*The Peshtigo Plutcher.*"

So, what is a plutcher?

When a person fishes a stream or river with caution and skill and direction, that person is a wader. Take that same person and see him slipping from rock to rock, wandering somewhat aimlessly, splashing his way through a stream, that person is a plutcher.

For several years, he was able pursue the life of *The Plutcher,* but as time and life went on, he found he enjoyed more than just wading around the Peshtigo River scaring the fins off trout. He found that he was more of a *putzer* than a plutcher.

And what is a putzer? A putzer is one who does many things—a little bit of this, a little bit of that—most of the time he has a little bit of this and that going on at the same time. A putzer is not an expert, but rather someone who gets by very nicely, for his own purposes, and above all has learned how to enjoy at least a little bit of every day, and tries to live each day fully. A description that our subject's better half says, "... is what he does best—putz!"

Thus, the once-*Peshtigo Plutcher* is now properly known as *The Peshtigo Putzer.*

So, who is *The Peshtigo Putzer,* and what can we expect from him?

First, although Putzer is a he, he is very attuned and appreciative of the shes in this world. (He married one 50 years ago and helped raise two more, plus a female dog, and now enjoys two she grandchildren. (There is one male grandchild and a son-in-law, so he is not totally outgunned.)

They own a place in Marinette County, on the Peshtigo River.

He enjoys perfect brandy or Wild Turkey Manhattans on his stoup (deck) overlooking the river, before supper.

He cooks (preferably outdoors).

He enjoys the outdoors, in most of the most common formats—fishing and hunting—but also takes pleasure in the silent sports—canoeing and cross-country skiing and biking and hiking and birding. (The Putzers do own a small fishing boat with a motor.) Regular exercise is not in his daily schedule unless he is locked to the computer for too long.

He is a moderate traditionalist. His fishing preference is with flies but he will not hesitate to drown a nightcrawler from the end of a cane pole. Most of his guns are small gauge and break open to see if a shell is inside, except for his muzzleloaders. He has found a fondness for blackpowder, but is still floundering with its real satisfaction level. When he bow hunts, he does so instinctively with a custom made recurve and two-blade broadheads.

He has no problem keeping fish for the grill, but not all. He will release all largemouth bass, but has a fantastic recipe for smallmouths, so he keeps his share.

Stream trout will be kept only for special occasions or if hooked too deep (rare with barbless flies). However the trout and salmon from Lake Michigan are very desirable.

Panfish, when of proper size, go for the pan.

He does not have the patience to catch walleyes.

A few northern pike measuring 24 inches or more will go for the pot, and two or three 14- to 16-inchers make a fine "herring."

Venison rates high on his list of palatable food as do grouse, wild turkey, and pheasant. One or two wood ducks are enough, especially if he gets lucky with a mallard or two. One Canada goose is plenty, and two, maybe three, squirrel make a good garlic and rice soup.

It usually takes a full season to find and procure these needs, and more often than not, much of his "shopping list" goes unfilled.

He doesn't own a dog, but enjoys a hunt with those who do, when invited.

He prefers the canoe to the boat. The only electronics on the boat are lights—but it does have oars, a rarity today.

From time to time he and his bride venture beyond Marinette County and out of state, but Wisconsin is home to them.

They camp occasionally, but "the cottage" in Marinette County has been their retreat for more than 50 years, so it gets priority.

In his retirement he writes, he photographs, he teaches, he works with wood. He tries to share what little he knows with others as a part of giving back, which he feels is a very important part of retirement. In other words, *he putzes.*

"And now, you know the rest of the story," as a famous radio personality says every day.

And, as these tales roll by, you will also know the rest of many stories revolving around this man, his family, and his friends as they "putz" their way through the outdoors of Marinette County and beyond.

Until we meet in, on, or near the river,
Keep a good thought!

The Peshtigo Putzer

BOOK I

Tales of The Peshtigo Putzer

"In Wishigan Country"

Although these tales are based in northeast Wisconsin, the stories can be appreciated anywhere there are lakes and streams and woods and fields and wildlife and people who enjoy the outdoors.

j.k.

The Putzers Ski

You don't like winter? Maybe you don't know how. Learn. The Putzers spend a late winter weekend in Wishigan Country, and I think you will agree, they know how to enjoy what others consider the worst of the four seasons.

Winter. For many, it is the longest of the seasons. But, if we will just learn from Mother Nature, winter is really the season of rest and rejuvenation. A time to heal wounds under the cover of snow.

Snow. Without snow a winter woods looks like a regiment of

skeletons standing erect, waiting for marching orders from Dr. Death.

Snow. The gauze and medication to heal a heavily used world of woods, water, marshes, and prairies.

Snow. What makes winter fun.

Once the ground has prepared itself to hold snow, and the white stuff covers it for more than a week, Putzer wants six inches of fluff, fresh and dry, every week, right up to the middle of March—then a nice slow, continuous change into spring can begin.

Snow, to Putzer, means cross-country skiing, snowshoe walks, some challenging photo opportunities, tracks that tell stories, and yes, the effort required to move it around from one place to another, so life can continue, on a regular basis, each day. The nice thing about snow is it comes with weather that is warm enough to continue outdoor cooking and enjoy the somewhat infrequent sunsets from the patio.

Putzer and his lady have been cross-country skiing since before it was popular. (No, not with mastodon bones. They're not that old.) However, their original equipment did consist of five-inch-wide slats mounted with "bear-trap" bindings that wrapped around and clamped onto hiking boots. And would you believe bamboo poles with seven inch baskets? (Believe it.) It may have been fun, but it sure was work!

Today they "schuss" on wax-less boards approximately two inches wide, with step-in bindings and fiberglass/graphite poles. Oh, P still owns, uses, and, as a matter of fact, prefers his waxables, wood with lignostone edges, but admits there are times when wax-less will work better—but not always. Snow conditions dictate when he uses what. The wax-less are for wet snow, so he doesn't have to use that sticky/gooey stuff called "Klister."

A good deal of their skiing is done near their home in southeastern Wisconsin, but when they visit Marinette County, in late February or mid-March, they like to use the trails off of

County Highway W, west of Crivitz. They also like those in Goodman Park, or they make their own tracks down the familiar old logging roads they walk and hunt during the other three seasons.

On this particular trip, Putzer had been retired for a little over two months. The girls: Mrs. P, daughter number one (by age), and grand-daughter number one (also by age) are going to celebrate Putzer's birthday in Marinette County.

Putzer proclaims he will leave a day early—much to the loudly verbalized chagrin of the ladies. (Mumble, grumble.) But he gets away with it.

When he arrives he finds sixteen inches of snow.

By the time the girls roll in on Friday night after work, they find shoveled paths and deck, a fire in the fireplace, and hot and cold running water.

"Well, as long as you were going to be here for the whole weekend, and I don't have to leave until Monday, I thought it was worth the effort," Putzer explained the luxuries.

The girls had to agree that maybe, just maybe, there was going to be some advantage to having at least one retired person in the family.

On Saturday they skied.

First they skied one of the more open trails west of Crivitz, off W. The sun had taken its toll, and the trail was marginal at best.

From there they drove north along Parkway Road and stopped to check out one of their favorite old logging roads. The road passes through old hemlocks and fifteen year old poplar, with maple and oak and lots of old and new white pine. When the road is followed to its end, it stops on the shores of the Peshtigo River.

The snow in the woods was much deeper than what they had encountered earlier, but it too was deteriorating. Mostly they skied along at a good pace, but occasionally they would break through the crust.

When they got to the river, they removed their skies and "walked." Well... not exactly.

The first step out of the bindings taught them how deep the snow really was—knee deep, for the adults. Ever try walking in waist deep snow? Granddaughter did. Fortunately, most of the time the crust held her, but once she almost dropped out of sight when she broke through a drift.

The river was beginning to open a little—not much. Just a spot or two behind the large protruding boulders where the current always swirled and boiled, even when covered with ice.

Spring was on its way.

"Hard to believe that in a month or so we'll be rafting," mused Putzer.

Back up on the ridge top it was time to take a lunch break.

After a snack of fruit and nuts washed down with ginger ale, and with the sun burning down, Putzer gave in to the natural turn of events—a nap.

He leaned his back against a tree, letting the sun warm his front side.

It wasn't a long snooze. Just enough for the chickadees to find and check him out—closely—from the toe of his boot.

The trip out was a little more difficult, because of the sun. Whatever crust had been strong enough to hold Putzer's weight earlier, was no longer there. He broke through continuously.

By the time they got to the truck, they were sweating but still laughing. Someone commented, "We'll sleep good tonight!"

Back at the cottage, they still had time to enjoy the sunset on the deck with a little liquid refreshment and cheese. Then Putzer got the grill going for burgers.

That night not only did they enjoy the fire in the fireplace, but they also were happy to have running water—both cold and hot. And yes, they did sleep good.

Truly, a weekend like this is what winter is all about—rest and rejuvenation. Mental rest from the pressures of daily jobs, and rejuvenation of the spirit, with fresh air, exercise, and good family quality time together for more than just a few hours.

Tomorrow, if the weather holds, they will canoe… but that's another story.

Until we meet in, on, or near the river,
Keep a good thought!

The Peshtigo Putzer

Snowshoes, Another Way to Enjoy Winter

Here Putzer is once again expounding on the virtues of winter. This time it is snowshoes. This scribe tries to fill in a few facts when P shifts gears, and, hopefully, between us we give you a good background; and, depending on the time of year you read this, perhaps the urge to get out on your own "agims."

It's hard to believe, but some people just don't like winter. They don't like the cold, and they really hate snow!" So were the words of the sage, Putzer, as we sat in front of a hot fire of oak and maple blazing away in the stone fireplace.

"I don't understand. Well, maybe a little I do, but not completely," he continued. "I mean, I guess I do have my limits when it comes to cold. I can be comfortable at zero, if there is little or no wind, but when the mercury drops below that I begin to not enjoy the outdoors as much as I want to—although we have spent a good six hours cross-country skiing at twenty-five to ten degrees below zero, one clear day in Minnesota. It was the only time I have used Vaseline to protect my skin, but we lived, enjoyed the day and the hot tub when we got back to the lodge," he rambled on. "I'll tell you about that some other time.

"What I don't understand is why people don't like snow! After all, snow is such a wonderful stratum, which covers an otherwise bland countryside with white, sparkling crystals of frozen water vapor; it is a healer; and it makes pretty pictures.

"Look out there," Putz pointed out the window where drifts flowed like smooth waves, and fresh flakes were making the entire scene trackless. "Have you ever seen anything more beautiful?"

For some reason, I am not sure why right now, Putz and I were discussing the merits of the white stuff and what you can do with it.

We spoke of, but were not always in accord with one another, on the subjects of skiing, and snowmobiling, and the best method for moving this beautiful ground cover from one place to another.

We agreed that one of the best times to study wildlife and learn about their travels and routines was to go tracking in winter.

I was about to interject that I enjoyed cross-country skiing, and found it a great way to enjoy a bright windless day, but I never got a chance.

"Snowshoes, that is what *this* winter is made for," P emphasized as he continued to stoke the hearth. "You talk about tracking, good old fashioned snowshoes are the best for that. Especially now, when the snow is over your knees."

I began to agree with him, but…

"You agree with what I am saying don't you? Of course you do, you've got a pair of 'shoes I'm sure.

"You know that the majority of men and women who own snowshoes prefer not to use them. They consider using them *work*—too big and bulky and heavy they say.

"Baloney! Weight is not the problem. Not knowing what type to use and when, that's the problem. You know, if people put as much time and effort into learning about snowshoes as they do into rods and reels and guns, and if they spent a little more money and had more than one pair, again like rods and reels and guns, the woods would be crawling with web walkers.

"On second thought, maybe it's just as well most people do feel the way they do. All the better for me and you. Right?"

He took a breath and then said, "Want a beer or soda or something? It's almost four o'clock. That's the cocktail hour you know. Mrs. P and your wife will be back soon. I'd better get the grill started. Pour us a Manhattan and add another log to the fire while I do that. OK? Thanks. Be right back!"

Off he went, and, naturally, I did what I was told. One does not argue, nor not do what is expected, when in the presence of a sage; but, man, I never cease to marvel how smoothly he shifts gears (subjects) all the time. (That is my take about what Mrs. P considers rambling talk that goes on and on and on.) We are, HE IS, deep in exalting the virtues of snowshoes, then shifts thoughts, and prepares to make supper. I'll bet, when he gets the grill going and returns, he will pick up the snowshoe conversation as if it was never interrupted, even momentarily.

Of course, he was right. The snow was beautiful, and tomorrow morning, if the sky cleared as predicted, we would be off to catch the early morning light. (The magic light, photographers call it. Warm light caught at limited moments, early and late in the day.) And I know a couple pairs of snowshoes will be in the back of the truck, because they are the best method to travel the countryside under these conditions, not only for tracking, but for stability when capturing an image on film.

I'm not sure if P knows this or not, but snowshoes are becoming more popular every year. Some say the sport is growing faster than cross-country skiing.

I have three pairs—an older set of Alaskans, a pair of Ojibwas, which I made a few years back from a kit, and a set of the high tech, aluminum/decked, 'shoes. Each has a purpose, but my preference is the Ojibs. Lighter, better designed with points fore and aft, like a double-end canoe. But they won't carry as big a load as the Alaskans, and when the snow has a crust or when crossing an icy section of lake, you can't beat the new models with crampons.

I am not certain when the snowshoe was invented; I have read it was about 6000 years ago. We know the Native American tribes had them by the time the "white eyes" came. And we know they had several sizes and designs for varying conditions and uses.

They used them to hunt buffalo. When the snow got so deep that the great beasts were literally plowing their way through chest high drifts, they, with the aid of their *"agim,"* (Ojibway for snowshoe) would walk on top of the snow and get right next to their quarry for an easy kill.

Even though I have three pairs, snowshoes are only a sometime thing for me. I use them when I have to. I would not like to be without them, but I am not a snowshoer for snowshoeing's sake. However, there is always one pair in the back of the truck once the snow flies.

Enough about me.

Putzer came back from igniting the grill as the girls returned from their shopping trip. They entered the house simultaneously.

"Well, where are those Manhattans I asked you to pour? What have you been doing?" Putz queried with a smile. "Now, you can add a couple of glasses of wine to the tray for the ladies."

"Just lost in thought," I said. "And I didn't want the ice to melt too much."

"And what were you daydreaming about now? What kind of

excuse to use so you don't have to shovel the snow when it stops, I suppose. Kids! Always trying to get out of a little work."

He accepted his glass and eased into his chair, and then, as if he had never left to light the grill, continued, "By the way, did you know that snowshoes are 6000 years old and......."

Until we meet in, on, or near the river,

Keep a good thought!

The Peshtigo Putzer

As Long as We Can't Ski

It is a very cold day in January. One even too cold for the Ps to venture forth and hit the ski trails, a rare day indeed, but they do occur. We get another glimpse of Putzer in his basement lair. He is again at the fly tying bench where, as he sorts and ties a few flies, he also relives a few days on the water.

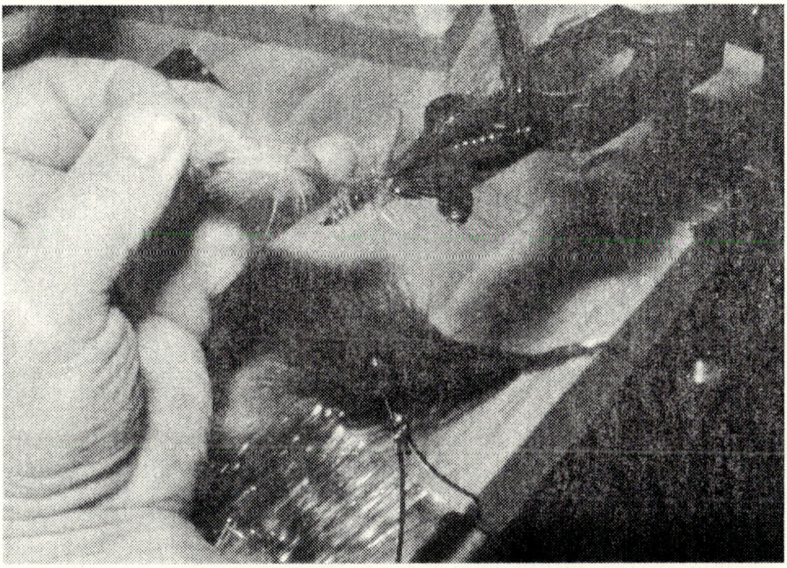

It's the middle of January, 2000. The Y2K problems have passed, the Rose Bowl is over and everyone in Wisconsin is happy with our Heisman Trophy-producing coach and team. The Super Bowl, on the other hand, holds no particular interest for Packer fans this year.

The temperature has dropped to below zero with the wind

whistling as it cuts around the corners and pushes through the pines. Even though the sun is out, the weather is a bit too harsh for Putzer and his bride to go skiing.

Mrs. P busies herself undressing the Christmas tree and repacking the inside house decorations in boxes for storage until next season. The stereo is playing a collection of holiday tunes for the last time for another eleven months.

Putzer heads for the basement. He gets a fire going in the wood burner. After a half hour of babying the small flickering flames and building them into blazing tongues leaping up the flue, the chill goes away. He can now add bigger, longer burning logs.

There is a down draft problem with this chimney and if it is not handled just right, the entire basement fills with smoke and then heads up the steps determined to engulf the entire house—a happening which Mrs. P does not enjoy!

Once the chill has gone and the stove is burning properly, Putzer goes over to the outdoor clothes rack and takes his fly vest off the hanger. Then he picks up the big Tupperware container with the rest of his fly fishing paraphernalia—reels, leaders, and an assortment of boxes full of flies. He empties the vest and the plastic container of their respective boxes and takes them to his fly tying bench. Here he begins to open each fly box, taking inventory to see what needs to be replaced.

The first box has nothing but Wooly Buggers in it.

Woolly Buggers are one of his favorite frauds. Well, *fraud* may not be the proper word. Fraud means "something that is not what it pretends." A Woolly Bugger doesn't really *pretend* to be anything in particular, but it does represent many things, so "impressionist" might be a better word.

The black W.B. is considered by many to be a fly *never* to be without. It can give the impression of being a leach or a giant stone fly, depending on how the fisherman presents it—or it can be anything else that is dark, alive, and tasty looking. When a W.B. is dressed in brown and orange, it becomes a crawfish;

white with a little pink, pieces of decayed salmon body floating back toward Lake Michigan after the fish has performed his/her ultimate duty of spawning. Purple seems to work well for black bass and so does olive green, even though neither color is representative of anything Putzer has ever seen swimming in the local waters.

Putzer has them all, plus several other color combinations of his own. He likes to keep three of each variety in his box. He needs a few replacements.

The next box has the Bugger's first cousin, the Woolly Worm. Actually, the Bugger is an offshoot of the Worm. It was the early Worm that begat the Bugger. Putzer thinks he will put the two patterns together in one box because they are so similar and he always has both in his vest all the time anyway; they can be used at any time for any species.

The Woolly Worm is tied smaller than the Bugger, on a short shank hook, with a short tag instead of the long marabou tail. Colors vary from the natural browns, greens, grays and black, to bright yellow and white. Generally, Putz ties them on a #8 nymph hook as opposed to the #4 streamer hook for the Bugger.

Another box holds bucktail and hackle streamers. Some put Buggers in the streamer category—Putzer does not. A streamer imitates, at least in size and form, bait fish—minnows and game fish still in the infant stage of life—or are tied to be used as attractors to stimulate strikes.

Putzer puts a lot of faith in streamers, more than most fly fishermen, especially for Peshtigo River bass and northern pike, but he is still looking for a pattern or two that will catch walleyes with regularity. He also likes small streamers for trout and panfish, especially crappie.

His standard patterns read like this: The Squirrel Tail (a fly of his own design); the Mickey Finn; an all black hackle wing, with a touch of silver here and there for sparkle, that he hasn't named yet because it still has not proved itself satisfactory—perhaps it needs tweaking, or maybe just a little more time; a Yellow

Blonde; the red and white Whisker Bug; the Black Ghost; and a constant flow of new experimental patterns that come and go as they do or do not catch fish.

There is a box for only terrestrials—hoppers, crickets, beetles, ants, and worms. A box for dry flies, one for poppers, another for Wiggle Bugs. One box holds nymphs and wet flies.

Then come the steelhead and salmon flies—Egg Sucking Leaches, Speys, and egg patterns of infinite variety.

One box, a rather large one, holds four extra large streamers plus one super long Wiggle Bug. Someday (always someday), Putzer hopes that these patterns, or at least one of them, will entice a musky to strike and he will be able to say he caught the mighty Muskellunge on a fly rod with a fly of his own making and design. Someday.

Then there are the specialty flies, which still must prove worthy of a place within a proven, categorized, established box (remember, this is 2000): the Wool-head Sculpin, a fly that simulates the bottom-hugging creature we seldom see but that can save the day on occasions when nothing else is working; the Deep Clouser Minnow, a relative newcomer that everyone has put into his/her box, including Putzer; Lefty's Deceiver, another newer creation by a well known "authority;" a shad pattern of Putzer's own design that has caught fish in Kansas; large, 1/0 long shank, blue and white, all white, and chartreuse and white streamers, all fitted with silver bodies and Flashabou® for Lake Michigan trout and salmon.

All of these are looked over and will be restocked as required. As each is viewed, Putz remembers.

"This pattern hasn't caught a thing and I don't understand why. It really looks good in the water. Here is a new pattern I haven't tried yet, picked it up on the Internet at *The Steelhead Site*, supposed to be good. This surface bug was a surprise; I caught a small walleye on it one morning. This pattern was my best for steelhead and salmon last season—and it was my own design."

On and on. Words spoken to himself as he continues to

examine and organize each box. The memories flowing smoothly, like the waters of the North Branch of the Pike.

Of course, the entire process of replacing flies will go on for more than just this day, but… "This has been a good start," Putzer says to no one in particular as he turns off the light on the bench and heads for the kitchen to see what he can put together for supper.

"It was a good day to begin this annual ritual. A nice way to spend a day in January—as long as we can't go skiing."

Until we meet in, on, or near the river,

Keep a good thought!

The Peshtigo Putzer

March—The Start of Canoeing Season

A rare and unusual visit to the Putzer Marinette County home—a pre-opener visit. Bring the drinking water, use river water for the toilet, turn up the heater, build a fire in the fireplace and enjoy the day, spend the night, go back home. This is not the season opener. This is a trip to scratch an itch. It does not happen often; the conditions must be just right.

March, the transition month. March, the month of promise. Putzer likes March, because he never knows what the month will bring him. Sometimes it is late skiing, some years an early steelhead run, always cooking in the sugarbush and the first redwing.

Of course, where you are in March has a lot to do with what you will be doing. If you live in the southern portion of Wisconsin, your chances of skiing are slim, and, conversely, if you live in northern Wisconsin, your chances of putting your boat in the water in March are not real high, but both can happen.

Take March 7, 1987 for example:

The Ps arrived on the 6th; early enough to open the cottage, get the fires going, haul a few buckets of water from the river, and still have time to enjoy the promising sunset. There was still snow in the woods, but the open, south facing slopes of the river bank were clear and dry. The path to Putzers' pier was open and dry, no shoveling required, albeit the pier was not yet in the water.

The sunset was deep—deep orange and red splashed on the few clouds that remained, with the deep blue sky in between. The scene was duplicated on the perfectly flat water of the river.

You should know that this portion of the Peshtigo is controlled by Wisconsin Public Service Corporation dams; and because of the everyday fluctuations of current and water level, the main stream of the river never really freezes solid enough to trust walking on it. Therefore, the river can be open at times of the year when other portions of this river, or other area rivers, are not. This explains why there was water to reflect the last rays of the day.

In the morning, after a walk and hearty breakfast of bacon, eggs, fried potatoes, and toast, and with the weatherman's promise of sun and 60-degree temperatures, the Putzers slipped their 17-foot Grumman double-ender into the river.

They paddled upstream, easing past closed cottages and silent resorts. How different it would be two months hence, when fishermen and sightseers would motor up and down the river, hour after hour, weekend after weekend.

With the sun shining, the wake up call to muscles that have been in semi-retirement for the past four to five months came easier.

There was still ice in the sloughs; only the main channel was open. The lakes were still frozen tight shore to shore, but the river itself was flowing strong. Soon critters would awaken and emerge from the mud, fish would begin to think about the reproduction process, avians would return from the south, and the river would be full of life.

The Ps paddled as far up as the river would allow. They beached the canoe and walked to the dam. The walk itself was an interesting experience—a combination of dry ground and fibula-deep snow, all along the same trail to the top.

At the dam the lake was, of course, frozen—how solid the Ps were not sure. Ice fishermen still drove their vehicles to their chosen locations, but water covered the entire surface.

"I wouldn't take my truck out there, not with water standing all over the place," P declared.

To which Mrs. P replied, "I wouldn't walk out there, even if you showed me the ice was three feet thick."

From their position at the top of the dam, they stood at the very summit of what was once, before the dam was built, the Peshtigo River's highest waterfall, Caldron, a 55-foot drop over a distance of 800 feet. Even with the dam in place, it was still gorgeous. Ice stalactites and stalagmites gleamed and glistened in the natural gorge before them. It was breathtaking.

After a brief shore lunch of sandwiches and Cokes they decided to see how far downriver they could paddle. It's about a two and a half mile stretch from the dam to the lake below. When they got to the lake they could only get about a quarter of a mile or so before they literally were "put on ice."

There they sat. Mrs. P, in the bow, rested on a dark honeycombed "beach." While Putz, in the stern, remained in water. An ice fisherman to their left was bent over, obviously hypnotized by a small hole in the ice. Honeycombed ice. All around him.

Mergansers, in the river, were dancing and squawking, courting, behind them; a mature bald eagle, white head gleaming almost gold now in the afternoon sun, soared overhead in search of supper.

"It just doesn't get any better than this," Mrs. P said. P agreed.

They paddled home. P grilled supper, and later, after a dying, half-hearted sunset, they built a new fire in the fireplace.

The next day was cloudy. A light rain was falling with a predicted high of 42 degrees. The Ps packed up and headed home.

Until we meet in, on, or near the river,

Keep a good thought!

The Peshtigo Putzer

Spring Is Made for Rafting

As we have seen, the outdoors, to the Putzers, means more than just fishing and hunting. We have seen that they ski and snowshoe when snow is on the ground. Now that the snow is almost gone, of course, their first thought is fishing. WRONG! At least for Putz, spring is more than fishing; it is adventure! Cold water thrills.

While spring always brings thoughts of love to Putzer, (love to hunt turkeys, love to fish for trout, crappies, bluegills) his thoughts also turn to rafting the Peshtigo.

For those not aware of what we have here in Wishigan Country, the Peshtigo River has the longest stretch of continuous whitewater in the state, perhaps the Midwest. Starting at the lower lip of Farm Dam, to the final ripple coming out of the last drop in Roaring Rapids, and a few minor hiccups beyond, you will find four-plus miles of humpy, bumpy rock gardens, and class I, II, III, and IV water, under normal river conditions. (The lower the class number, the easier the ride.) In early spring those numbers can, and do, rise to V's and VI's.

One such trip stands out in Putzer's mind.

It is April, right around the 20th. Saturday is a work day at the cottage, but Sunday is planned to run the Peshtigo with Putzer's two buddies. Lady P. doesn't raft until the water temp is at least 65 degrees or more, which means July—if the water is high enough.

The three "guys" meet at Kosier's for the morning run. They wear their own wet suits, wool sweaters, windbreakers, helmets, PFDs, and tennis shoes. All they require from the outfitter is a paddle and a raft.

As expected, the river is high, but not excessive. They talk Danny, the raft company's owner, into letting them run by themselves in one of the smaller rafts. Everyone else is in the big boats with a guide.

Everything is going along just fine. The takeoff at Farm Dam is smooth. The first section is exhilarating. A good warm-up. Soon they approach Roaring Rapids.

For those who have never rafted in spring, the name Roaring Rapids does not do this portion of the river justice. To the adjective *roaring*, one must add words like: **"thundering, booming, resounding."**

After running First Drop, they do the usual body surfing, an activity done only during the spring trips.

Body surfing is done by walking out on an underwater rock ledge, then lying back so you go over the drop feet first. The farther out into the river you walk, the longer the trip.

A normal surf involves going over the drop, then getting submerged twice under waves, and ending up in calm, shallow water where you walk to shore.

After the two waves, when you pop up above the surface,

you grab a needed breath of air before standing up.

Putzer, on his third trip out on the ledge, walks to the farthest edge and takes off. He hits the drop with a yell, submarines the waves and as he rises, opens his mouth for that big gulp of air.

One problem—by going out farther than normal, a third wave comes into play. Instead of air, after the expected second wave, Putzer takes in a huge mouthful of 40-degree water as he gets pulled under for the unexpected third time.

As the water goes down his throat, past his lungs, he feels a pain like nothing he has felt before—cold water passing the warm lungs. This is not a good thing! Fortunately, it is a strong wave that has not developed a liking for wetsuits and helmets, so it gets rid of Putzer quickly.

Having been taken completely by surprise, Putzer lies back in the quiet water to rest—and breathe. From the corner of his eye he sees the guides talking and looking his way. One guide gets ready to jump in to "rescue" him.

Putzer sits up, waves an arm, "I'm okay," he assures them, then heads for the shallow water and shore.

Back in the raft, the "musketeers" continue on their way. Over Second Drop, and out, then on to Third Drop. Down Third Drop... but not out!

What?

Third Drop decides to detain the trio.

They are caught in a back hydraulic.

The raft, filled with water, moves forward, then is drawn back, pulling the guys under the falls... then moves them out again, and back... forward and back.

Try as they may, they cannot break free.

They paddle, they stand and paddle, they stand, lean, and paddle—all three at the same time. Nothing. Just back under the falls and out again. Back and out.

The guide yells at them to bail out of the raft and get to shore.

They "... can't hear you."

Finally, the river says, "Enough!" and "spits" the raft free from the falls, continuing them on their way. Within less than fifty feet, they plunge over Five Foot Falls full of water.

After getting to shore and emptying their "donut," the rest of the trip is "... a piece of cake."

Back at the landing, now in dry clothes and having a hot drink, Danny says to the three of them, "That's the last time I let you or anyone else go in small rafts when the river is this high. I hope you learned your lesson."

"Oh yeah," says Putzer, "and I also lost my wedding ring. My finger must have shrunk and it must have slipped off in the cold water."

So, if anyone reading this is fishing or rafting or just messing around in the Roaring Rapids section of the Peshtigo, and happens across a plain gold ring with the inscription, "10/6/56," on the inside, please return it to *Wishigan Outdoors*, Attention: Putzer. Thanks.

Until we meet in, on, or near the river,

Keep a good thought!

The Peshtigo Putzer

About Waterspouts and Whirlwinds... and Canoes

The Putzers head out on one of their favorite springtime "adventures"—paddling the still-barren river into the lake—birding and viewing wildlife. Little did they know what kind of adventure they would really experience.

It was one of those gorgeous spring days in April, the 30th to be exact (but not this past 30th). The temperature along the river at six a.m. was 25 degrees Fahrenheit, by noon it was 75. A perfect day for a paddle.

Mrs. P and Putzer loaded their "viewing gear"—binoculars,

cameras, field guides, *and a few snack items*—into the old Grumman, and let the current catch hold of the 17-foot canoe as they pushed off from the pier. This would be a day of drifting and dipping the paddles in a very leisurely manner. A day to catch a few rays, as they say, and see what the warm winds had brought recently to Wishigan Country.

The sky was perfectly clear. If a cloud even thought of existing it was somewhere to the west, perhaps Minnesota; and, because they were on the Peshtigo, there was no way for the Putzers to know if Minnesota had clouds or not; and, if the truth be known, not that they wanted to slight Minnesotans, but today, they really didn't care.

Mostly, they meandered with the current, but every now and then they would veer into, or cut across, areas otherwise filled with weeds, which would normally prevent this type of exploration. Here, this time of the year, was where the first signs of renewed life appeared—in the shallows. Were the bluegills making ready to spawn—creating little circular "beds"? Are the turtles and frogs out of the mud? Any northern pike snoozing in the sun?

They would also explore the little creek that flowed into the main stream, looking for migrant song and shore birds. Now, before the leaves sprout and unfold, is a perfect time for spotting the little warblers and wrens that otherwise can only be heard as they flit through the alder and other streamside brush. This is also the time and place to see sandpipers, snipe, and both lesser and greater yellow legs.

On the lake the Putzers hoped to catch hooded mergansers in their courting mode and to check out the eagle's nest.

As they made one final cut before entering the lake, Putz said to Mrs. P, "Look at the water ahead of us."

It was as if someone had dropped a clear piece of Plexiglas into the river, perpendicular to the surface. On one side, the Putzers' side of the "shield," the water was perfectly flat and calm, while on the other side of the "window" there were foot-high waves.

No sooner had the words left his mouth, than the wind came roaring from across the lake in front of them, high in the tree tops. It, the wind, bounced off the riverbank to their right, and charged across the water to the bank on the left, behind them. As it hit the left bank of trees, it ricocheted down to water level, where it became a twirling, whirling, wet funnel. It looked capable of sucking up everything in its way that it could grab. A waterspout! And it was heading directly toward the canoe.

I believe it is proper here if I step away from this treatise and give a short explanation as to what the Putzers experienced and perhaps why. I have used the word "waterspout," perhaps I should have called it a whirlwind.

"Whirlwind: a rapidly whirling, small-scale vortex of air, often seen on hot still days," so says David M. Ludlum, in the "THE WEATHER BOOK."

Whirlwinds are formed when contrasting temperatures, like cold water and unusually warm air, converge. The overheated layer of air rises suddenly, creating a swirl. (The same conditions the Putzers experienced.)

Whirlwinds, of the type described in the story, have only a minimum of danger (the Putzers didn't know that), but still should not be taken lightly (which they didn't). The water seen in the spout is mostly condensation, instead of water being sucked up from the surface.

Whirlwinds can be a few feet to perhaps thirty feet wide and five to one-hundred feet tall. Larger spouts would be classified as waterspouts, which can be several hundred feet wide and thousands of feet high. Do not put whirlwinds, waterspouts, and tornados in the same context. Though similar in appearance, waterspouts are not as powerful as tornados, and whirlwinds are not as powerful as waterspouts.

Whirlwinds, as the Putzers experienced, are sometimes referred to as "fair weather spouts," and are short lived, two to fifteen minutes. They are more likely to be seen while traveling across a desert, where they are called "dust devils," than they are on the Peshtigo River.

Now that you know more than you ever wanted to know about what the Putzers were encountering, I'll return to the tale.

It wasn't a big spout as spouts go, perhaps ten to fifteen feet in diameter and eight to thirty feet at its tallest. It kept changing size, going up and down, as it came within twenty feet or less from the bow of the canoe, where Mrs. P sat.

P didn't know what to do first, grab his camera for a really great picture, or paddle the heck out of there.

He looked at his wife.

In her own words, later, "I was hanging onto the canoe for dear life yelling, 'My God Putz, which way is that thing going?'"

Her knuckles were pure white and the gunnels were in danger of being reshaped.

Putz grabbed his paddle. Before he could put the paddle in the water to move them away, "that thing" shifted again, and moved away from them. He dropped the paddle and grabbed his camera, snapping off two quick shots just as the vortex was leaving the river. It hit the far bank with very little power, and was gone.

The entire event, from seeing the sharply defined edge on the water until the spout left the river, took less that a minute—much faster than the telling. If Putz had not made those "grab shots," he might not be real sure that it wasn't all only a dream.

But it wasn't a dream.

Had it been a dream, he would never be able to explain the little warp, with the permanently imbedded fingerprints, in the bow gunnels of the Grumman.

Until we meet in, on, or near the river,

Keep a good thought!

The Peshtigo Putzer

Author's note: Information on whirlwinds come from Paul Joseph, meteorologist at WTMJ in Milwaukee; THE AMERICAN WEATHER BOOK, by David M. Ludlum; WORLD OF THE WIND by Slater Brown; POWERS OF NATURE, National Geographic Society; and THE WORLD BOOK ENCYCLOPEDIA.

A Special Place

Some places just don't appear to be special, and mostly aren't. That is unless you know when to visit them. Here is one such unlikely place.

We all have special places for special times—quiet times. Times to think, meditate, enjoy what God has created.

Everyone should have such a place. I do; so does Putzer. Actually, Putzer and I share several special places scattered through out our state—Wisconsin.

One such place we share is in Wishigan Country. It is an unlikely place, really; a segment of blacktop road in front of the Putzer cottage. Only three miles long, we use merely a tad more than one mile of that distance. *And,* it is only special *very early* in the morning, just prior to, and as the sun rises; before most people are out of bed—off and running.

Mostly, it is more special when traveled alone, but certain people, people like the Putzers, can share the place because they are compatible when together at a place like that. As I have said, I also have shared this section of road with the old sage—a privilege I hope never to lose.

What makes this road so special?

Every time we walk it early, Mother Nature always provides something to see and hear. Sometimes a flock of wild turkeys will cross ahead of us, sometimes a bear. Perhaps a pileated woodpecker will squawk and hammer out a "Good morning!" We never know. That is what makes it, always, real quality time—in other words, special.

Like the morning of August 21, 1995.

I stopped by the night before on my way to the U.P. to do a little research for a story I was writing. Mrs. P, who was back home, asked me to, "... please check up on the old boy, because he was a bit under the weather when he left." (He was just fine. "... needed a bit of time alone, that's all.")

Anyway, it's a reasonably clear morning, only a few high cirrus clouds. Putz's English breakfast tea and Oreo cookie breakfast, in front of the picture window that overlooks the Peshtigo River, is finished.

The thermometer indicates a light flannel shirt to start our walk, but the glow in the east promises a warm day. Putz gathers up an appropriate shirt for each of us, I pick up the camera, and we stroll into the morning.

"Putz's " section of road is empty—empty and wet. Everything is covered with dew. The wet seeps through the canvas portion of my shoes and into my socks as I wander off the blacktop to shoot (photograph) the tops of wet grass seeds, glistening, frost-like, in the not-yet-sunrise light.

"I told you to put on your L.L.'s. You kids will never learn," chides P, as he sees my wet feet.

A little further along, at the crest of the hill where the road drops down toward the creek, stand two of this year's fawns—still in spots.

"Now if you two... will just stand quietly... while I take your picture..." I speak in a very soft, unalarming voice. And wonder of wonders, they do. Their curiosity this morning must be aroused by something unusual, for they keep staring, even after the camera mirror and shutter go "whack, whack," and the motor drive "whirls" with each exposure.

"Must be my hat," states Putzer.

"Always said I'd rather be lucky than good," I say to Putz after the twins leave.

"Now, that's my line, and you know it," he replies. "I guess I'll take that as a compliment."

Turning off the main blacktop and heading up a dead-end road, I find a perfect example of what photographers look for—mood light.

On the right, there is goldenrod still in shadow—leaves dotted with dew. The image is soft, muted. Meanwhile, on the left, where the early sun has already collided full force with the flowers of a similar patch of goldenrod, the leaves are already dry. This portrait becomes a glowing, vibrant contrast of deep gold against even deeper green. Of course, I stop to capture the moment on each side of the road.

Putz points out a shot angle I do not see. (As it turns out, it becomes the best of the series. "Of course," states P upon seeing the shots weeks later, "Why would it not be?")

Near the creek, a swamp milkweed shows its deep, dusty-pink flowerhead and its rusty-red stems; goldfinch are feeding on thistle heads that have already turned to seed.

The sun is higher now; it has lost its early morning warmth of color. The magic light is gone.

The morning has, however, gotten much warmer in terms of temperature. The flannel shirts come off, and we wrap them around our waists.

Putzer picks up a discarded plastic bag, which he will use to hold other roadside trash we will find on our return trip. The bag will be full by the time we get back.

The first car of the morning rushes by with a ***"Swoosh,"*** boat trailer in tow.

"From its speed it must be late for its blind date with the fickle fish," says P, with a slight chuckle.

Our special time and place is gone. It has become just another blacktop road going from point A to point B.

Back at the cottage I put on the coffee as Putz starts breakfast.

This day has begun, as it does many times throughout the year, with the early morning walk. And each morning I, or we, or they, walk this walk, and even though the feet travel the same paths, there is always something new. Each season brings forth different forms of wildlife and events, always from a different perspective.

I thank God for this special time at one of my special places—*Putzer's road.*

Until we meet in, on, or near the river,
Keep a good thought!

The Peshtigo Putzer

One Man's Quest,

and a woman's patience

Here is a perfect example of how Mrs. P humors, tolerates, perhaps even mollifies Putz when he gets a thought, idea, "plan" in his head. She goes along, generally, for two reasons: so he doesn't hurt himself, and because she doesn't want to miss anything.

Have you ever gone on a quest? Putzer has. Well, at least it was a quest for him. For his wife, I'm not so sure.

Before we go too far, this, I think, would be a good time to define the term *quest*, so we are all on the same playing field, or in this case, all paddling the same stream.

To quest: 1. a search or pursuit made in order to find or obtain something. 2. an adventurous expedition, as by knights in medieval romances. 3. those engaged in such an expedition. So says RANDOM HOUSE COLLEGE DICTIONARY, 1996.

So, was this a quest? Certainly the Putzers did search, and there was *"romance,"* as long as you keep the word's meaning in the context of *"adventurous expedition."* With those thoughts in mind, indeed, it was **"A Quest!"**

Our story begins a long, long time ago—pre-Putzer wedding. Putzer's not-yet-father-in-law and he were stealing a few hours away from building the cottage, and were grouse hunting. (The cottage, by the way, was a very good incentive for P to be seriously pursuing marriage to this only child and heir to said property.)

The two stopped for lunch at Twelve Foot Falls County Park. It was, and still is, a very popular spot both for trout fishing and the beauty of the falls.

(I saw a wedding performed here once; the bride and groom positioned themselves so the waterfall was behind them and they were surrounded by evergreen trees. The falls became an animated stained glass window behind the temporary altar the group had brought with them. That little corner in the park became the chapel. But I digress—again.)

Somewhere, during the lunchtime conversation, Putz's N-Y-F-I-L said, "You know, there is supposed to be an even bigger falls upstream from here."

"Really?"

"Yup."

"You know how to get there?" P asked, thinking of maybe getting some photos that very few people had ever taken.

"No, and it's not on the map either," was N-Y-F-I-L's reply, while pulling out his well-used Marinette County map. He unfolded it on the picnic table and, with his finger, traced upstream from where they were.

"Well, I sure don't see anything indicating a falls," P declared.

"That's what I said. It ain't on no map."

After lunch they followed a narrow trouter's trail upriver, but it only led a short distance, into tag alder full of old-man's-beard. They found no grouse either, so the subject was dropped.

Still, the thought of another falls, one not readily seen or photographed intrigued Putz, so somewhere in his subconscious he filed away the thought that the best way to get to this waterfall, someday, would be by canoe.

He had a canoe.

Over the years, after the wedding, they, the entire family, would have lunch at the park occasionally, and when time allowed they would half-heartedly look for paths leading to the mythical falls upstream, but they never found anything promising.

But, the thought persisted. Putzer kept his eyes on magazines for photos of the falls, but found none.

He broached the subject with a publisher friend who specialized in Wisconsin stories and photos.

"Yes, they tell me there is a taller falls above Twelve Foot. I've never been there. Nor have I ever seen any photographs of it. If you go, let me know; maybe we can go together. We will go *questing*." he said. "It will be a wonderful way to spend the day."

Several times they attempted to get together, but it never happened.

Finally, years—think decades—later, Putzer told Mrs. P, "I am going to find that falls and photograph it! ***I have a quest!*** If my friend's schedule and mine can't get together, I will go alone! I will put in above Twelve Foot Falls and paddle upstream until I find this 18-foot, or whatever size, falls that is supposed to be there, and I will bring back photos to prove its existence.

"According to the county map, I have several miles of stream to paddle until I hit the next road crossing; it has to be in between the two roads somewhere. I will plan on being gone the better part of a day."

"I'm going along," Mrs. P said. (She's real good that way. She usually doesn't care where he's going as long as she goes too. It works for them.)

They went.

(At this point I feel I must explain that even though the actual "quest" took place years after the original idea was filed into Putzer's data bank, he still used the old map—the one his father-in-law used. Maps don't normally change much and Putzer is always adding notes and markings to it, as I am sure many of you do too. Also, at the time, Putzer did not own a WISCONSIN ATLAS & GAZETTEER, although it was on the market. I make this statement only for those who might take the time to look into the GAZETTEER and see that Eighteen Foot Falls is well-identified. Had Putzer had said book at the time, it would have been a short trip. And no story.)

Thus, all said and explained, I take you now to the day of ***The Quest.***

Of course, the day is cloudy. It always is when Putz takes his camera, but this time, even if it rains, they will not be stopped. Their, ***his***, quest was now almost a crusade.

The portage from the parking lot to a put-in spot above Twelve Foot Falls is only about one hundred yards. Shouldering the Old Town, P weaves and stoops his way through an edge of cedar woods next to the pool at the base of Twelve Foot Falls. Stepping through mud and over fallen trees, climbing dark, lichen-spotted rock, and inching and pushing through tag alder and tall grass down a narrow path, P reaches the water's edge.

Lowering the canoe to the ground P finds an old friend and associate, a wood tick, working its way up his pant leg. "It must be spring," he says to no one special.

Returning for additional gear and his paddling companion, he runs into a group of Boy Scouts. They exchange greetings, and their leader, having seen him carrying the canoe, asks what they are going to do. P tells him of his quest. The leader gives P an odd look and says, "Why don't you just drive to it? There's a road just a short distance north of here."

They were walking as they talked, and P stumbled over the log he was crossing as the leader told him about the road.

"Ex... excuse me," Putzer stammered. "Did you say, drive to the falls?"

"Sure. They put a road in to it last fall. It doesn't go right up to the falls, but it's not much of a walk. That's our next stop."

How was he to know? Now what? Should they stop? Should he tell his better half? All these thoughts zipped through his mind at the speed of light—dim light.

This, of course left P with a dilemma, should he tell his wife about the road? A road that led to the falls he had wanted to find for years. Or should he just go on with his original plan—to venture forth, paddles in hand, into the unknown of the North Branch of the Pike River?

For him, it was really a no-brainer. ***He had a quest!*** It has been in his mind too long to toss aside now.

"*Never!* I *want* to do this," Putzer said to himself.

Undaunted he continued.

"Thanks for telling me," he said to the scout leader. "But we'll just paddle up there anyway."

The leader shrugged his shoulders. Scouts are taught to be courteous.

Putz continues to debate with himself about telling Mrs. P, and decides it is only fair to let her know what he has learned.

After everything was tucked into the canoe and they had pushed off, he says casually, "Oh, by the way, one of those guys over there with the kids, he said you can drive to Eighteen Foot. How about that."

"Yes, I know; I talked to him too," was her reply, without turning her head.

The North Branch of the Pike River above Twelve Foot Falls is deep, tannic acid brown, and flows between thick bushy alder and willow banks. "Someday I should bring the canoe back here and fish this," Putzer says. "I really don't think this stretch of the river gets much, if any, pressure."

"Another someday?" Mrs. P. replies. "You will never have enough somedays the way you react to everything you see. Someday this, someday that. All I hear is 'someday'."

Putzer does not reply.

They paddle upstream for maybe a half mile and run into an old beaver dam which, through the years, had accumulated a lot of additional debris. Except for a break on the left side, it could have been a bridge—it was that large and sturdy.

"You want to turn around and go back?" asks Mrs. P.

Putzer is taken a little back, surprised. He thinks to himself, "Apparently there is some thought about the saneness of this undertaking, now that we know about the road."

"Not really," he replies to the question. "We've gone this far, it can't be much farther if it is only a mile or so by road like the scoutmaster said. We'll keep going."

They pushed and pulled their way over the dam. They were actually standing and walking on it.

Mrs. P says very little. She almost does a half-gainer into the creek when the canoe *tilts a tad* as P is *steadying* it for her while she is climbing back into her seat.

"You OK?"

"I'm fine."

"Good."

The next few minutes are paddled in absolute silence.

Ahead they hear the falls, or at least some kind of fast water. They beach the canoe in a little sandy, worn spot. A place obviously used by trout fisherman. A path leads up a steep bank of granite "steps." There it meets another path. The noise, and falls, is to the right. The path leads to the top of Eighteen Foot Falls.

After viewing the falls from above, they backtrack and find a small parking lot. Indeed there is a road. Indeed they could have driven, but...

Mrs. P returns to the falls, while Putz goes back to the canoe to paddle across to the opposite bank to see if he can find a better vantage point to photograph the falls head-on.

There are no worn spots for easy access on this side. He grabs hold of some alder and steps gingerly onto as firm ground as possible. Pulling the canoe as far onto shore as he can, he secures it with rope, hoists the camera gear to his shoulders and heads upstream. (It should be noted here that P is using a 4x5 camera, not 35mm. Which is the reason he "... hoists the camera gear to his shoulders...")

The path is narrow, not like the one on the other side. This is a leaf-covered deer trail, not man-worn. There are no little side trails leading to the water's edge. Again he muses to himself, "Not much fishing pressure from this side; should have brought my waders and tackle."

Eighteen Foot Falls is not a come-to-the-edge-and-drop-straight-down type of falls, not a lot of Marinette County falls are. Rather, Eighteen Foot drops over a series of hard igneous rock steps—natural fish ladders. Salmon would have no trouble negotiating upstream. I am willing to bet that brook trout climb the watery rungs in fall when they look for suitable spawning places.

Below the cascading whitewater lies a large pool, which is part of the bend in the river as it continues twisting, turning, serpentining its way in the general direction of south and east, down to the mighty Menominee, and eventually into Green Bay.

Putzer takes a picture or two, not because of great lighting, but because he is here. *This is why he came! His quest is complete.* If the results aren't the best, (and they weren't) he can always return (he has)—*via the road.*

Returning to the canoe, he re-crosses the stream and picks up his paddling buddy.

The return trip was a pleasant one, drifting with the current, only using the paddle as a rudder. Even the old beaver dam was negotiated with ease. The warblers were nesting and active, and although photographically the trip was marginal at best, the day was still great.

So there you have the story of one man's quest and his consort's willingness to oblige his middle-aged madness.

Really…it was a wonderful day!

Until we meet in, on, or near the river,

Keep a good thought!

The Peshtigo Putzer

His First Musky

There is nothing as exciting as your first musky! Putzer's came a bit unexpectedly, plus he had a little "help"—sorta. The help actually added to the excitement—in a way. Now the big question is: Did P keep his first musky? Would you today, if you were in P's place? Would he?

Nice stringer of fish you got there," the young man complimented Putzer. "You better release them soon though, or they might die. A couple of them don't look so good as is. Why have you kept them so long?"

"Well, if you must know, I have no intention of releasing these fish. It has been a while since I had myself a good fresh fish fry and these Smallies will do just fine," Putzer replied.

The young man started to open his mouth and was about to give the old man a mild reprimand, but he never got the chance.

"Young man, I know you don't approve of this, but let me tell you, there was a time when people used to fish not only for fun, but for the wonderful meal their catch would provide."

(**Gasp!** The "kid" is taken back.)

Putzer continued, "Back then a fish fry could be any day of the week, not only on Fridays, and the fish would be fresh caught, and that included *trout and muskies*."

(**Triple gasp!!**)

"Of course, I realize those were medieval times," Putzer continued. "Why, would you believe it? Everyone was called a *fisherman*, and that included women and children, and no one was ever offended. It was a time when *electronics* meant carrying a flashlight. In case you are wondering, we are talking about the late 1960's," Putzer concluded.

The young man just stood on the bow of his newly-purchased bass boat, dumbfounded. Finally he stammered, "Th...th... thanks for clearing that up. Are you trying to tell me that you really kept trout and muskies to eat?"

"Sure! Muskies are great baked on a grill," P volunteered.

With that the "kid" cranked up the motor and moved away, shaking his head.

Putzer looked on as the boat disappeared downriver. It had been a long day. He eased into the bank, found a soft, mossy place, and stretched out under the shady tree. He would rest a bit before returning home.

Soon he was way off somewhere in the past, 1968, opening day…

Opening morning finds Putzer on an upper stretch of the Peshtigo. Fishing is good. By ten o'clock he has five trout in the creel.

Sunday morning is a copy of Saturday, and Putzer is back at the cottage early enough to take a short canoe ride before returning home.

He eases the canoe into the water. The faint current catches the bow of the canoe as he floats away from the pier.

He selects an old white, with a black stripe, Flatfish to cast and troll. He notices a slight fraying in the line, but for some reason ignores it.

Casting directly behind the canoe, P begins to paddle and troll. The quiver in the rod leaning against his leg tells him that the crescent shaped plug is doing its job.

Putzer finds trolling relaxing. It gives the mind time to wander and ponder, as well as the opportunity to view a lot of wildlife. The method also catches fish.

A woodpecker hammers its nose into a nearby tree looking for brunch. The yellow-greens of aspen, soft whites of chokecherry, and subtle, yet deep, dirty reds of the maple flowers color the shore. "Who says that autumn is the only season with color?" he thinks to himself.

A doe looks up sharply from her drinking, then bounds into the woods. "Soon you will have young to care for—maybe even twins," says Putzer to the pretty four-legged lady.

"Click! Click! Click!" The reel speaks. Snag. Back paddle and unhook the plug.

Putzer glances at his watch; it's noon—time to head back.

He flips the flatfish into a small pocket of stumps and rocks, a place from which he has taken a northern pike from time to time.

The plug floats motionless on slack line while he picks up the paddle. At the first draw, as the canoe moves forward, the plug begins its slow tantalizing side-to-side descent.

Click! Click! Click!

"Nuts! I caught that stump!" Putzer says out loud.

Slowly, he raises the rod with one hand while bringing the paddle on board with the other. No snag this time. There is something moving on the other end of that line.

It doesn't fight hard, just confidently swims up river, as if it had just picked up a small part of lunch, an hors d'oeuvre perhaps. It is not a small fish. If it is a walleye, it is huge. If a northern pike, very respectable. Putzer figures a northern.

Then it rolls close enough to see the smooth, iridescent, emerald green sides, and those yellow eyes. Eyes that leer at him before returning to the bottom of the river.

A muskie! He has never caught a muskie before—not even a little one. This is no wall-hanger, but it will be his first—if he can land it.

Then he remembers that he didn't use a leader, the frayed line, and that he has no net.

"Too late now," he sighs.

Gradually, P works the fish back to the canoe. As he comes within a rod's length, Putzer slips his hand into the water and *sloooowly* draws the fish over it. He had read somewhere that a fish will relax if you stroke its belly, thereby making it easy to grab. Maybe that will work somewhere, but not here. At the first touch, it is gone... but not off. This is becoming a difficult situation.

Just then two young boys come up river. Putzer shouts to them and asks if they have a net.

No.

He asks if they would please push him in to shore so he has a chance to beach the fish. The oldest boy, perhaps seventeen, picks up the oars and with great skill and caution *eases* the nose of their boat into the belly of the canoe, then *gently* pushes it to shore.

Within the short span of time that it takes for the two craft to meet, disaster almost strikes—the younger boy, perhaps seven, leans over the bow of their boat, and as the fish passes, tries to grab the line in an effort to help land it. He means well.

(Now Putzer is generally a calm individual; he doesn't excite easily, but when that kid almost loses his fish, he tells him to keep his hands inside of his own boat. He explains that he is quite capable of losing his own fish and doesn't need anyone's assistance. He must have been quite persuasive, or maybe just a little excited, because the young man snapped back, sat in his seat, and never moved a muscle or spoke another word.)

As soon as the canoe gets next to shore Putzer bounds out with all the grace and agility of a pregnant cow. He loses a shoe, and almost goes nose over belly, head first, in the process. There he is, a grown man prancing around on wet, moss-covered rocks with one shoe on and one shoe off, just like *Diddle, Diddle Dumpling My Son John*.

While he is hopping around his mind does a strange thing. It blanks out all thoughts of the fish. All he can think of is that he is off balance and looking silly bouncing around in only one shoe. So he kicks off the other shoe. He is now balanced.

Through some miracle, the fish is still on and getting pretty pooped, as is Putzer. Slowly, very carefully, with steady tension, P brings the fish toward the rocky shore. Putzer can see that if the musky were allowed to make one more run, even a feeble one, it would be gone.

One tiny hook is all that remains between capture and freedom, and that hook isn't going to hold much longer.

It is now or never! Putzer thrusts his right hand toward the exposed, red gills groping for something to grab; at the same time his left arm stretches back in an effort to maintain slight tension on the line. The right hand finds the narrow strip of flesh between the gills.

Putz clamps down hard and heaves. His knuckles feel as if they are being drawn cross-grained against a rasp. It is a bad grip so he drops his rod and switches hands. Now the fish is his!

With heart pounding and hands hurting, with the fish in one

hand, he picks up his rod and shoes, and puts everything back into the canoe. He thanks the boys for their help and apologizes for yelling at them earlier. They make some pleasant remarks about his catch and take off.

For the next few minutes he just sits there looking at the glistening jewel spread out on the bottom of the canoe. His hands are still in the gills, crimson rivulets of blood run down the emerald sides—most of which is Putzer's. P looks for a stringer. There is none.

He is about to tie the fish to the anchor rope when his father-in-law comes motoring by. Putzer hails him over to ask for a tow and show off a little. F-I-L comes along side, takes one look, and says, "Walk!" Then he motors away.

But he comes back, and Putzer and the musky arrive safely home.

Putzer awakens slowly.

"Wow, what a dream, just like it was yesterday," he says to himself. "I wonder, what I would do if I caught that musky today? Take a photo and release it, I guess. After all that's what we do. Right? Surc."

Putzer rubs his chin considering the question. Hummmm... baked on the grill... hummmmmmm...

You be the judge.

Until we meet in, on, or near the river,

Keep a good thought!

The Peshtigo Putzer

Mrs. P Adjusts to Retirement

For readers who have followed this trivel over the years, you know that Putzer retired a few years before Mrs. P. Finally, Mrs. P said, "Enough!" And so it was. This is how they spent the first time they had the opportunity to go to the cottage since that final day of employment of Mrs. P.

It was the Putzers' first trip into Wishigan Country since they were both in the retired mode. Mrs. P had actually retired a few weeks earlier, but, having other priorities, the trip north had to wait. P had sneaked in a trip "... to do some chores." (And catch a few fish.) But Mrs. P had "... too much to catch up on." (Like lunches.)

They drove up on a Monday. (No more weekend traveling for them if they could help it.) The normal three-hour, 160-mile trip took 210 miles and six hours—they had a few side stops to make along the way—but, hey! They have no real time restraints now, so who cares?

After settling in, they eased the canoe into the water and took a leisurely paddle up river to look at the damage done by a fire to the local restaurant. They found it totaled.

"Think they will rebuild?" Mrs. P inquired.

"That's what I hear."

Now, normally the Ps would have fished as they paddled. They did have the rods along and Mrs. P did try a few casts, but it was windy and cold, so they kept the trip short and settled for a fire in the fireplace instead. (P did grill burgers out, however. It is a very rare occasion when the weather gets so bad that Putz won't cook out.)

Tuesday morning it was thirty-six degrees outside, fifty-eight inside, at five a.m. Putz started a little warming fire in the fireplace, and cranked up the thermostat on the heater.

By seven o'clock P had had his second cup of tea and cookies in front of the big window overlooking the river. Mrs. P arose as P popped the second Orco.

"Morning. Thought maybe you'd sleep in this morning," Putz mumbled through the crumbs.

"Don't talk with your mouth full. Still not into sleeping in. Maybe I never will be. Let's go for a walk."

As they step outside, a turkey gobbles. Twice. Close.

"That's a nice way to start the morning," says P.

"He is welcoming me to retirement," replies Mrs. P.

The Ps walk through the "back yard" and check out the young spruce they planted several years ago, and the wild blueberries.

"The spruce are doing fine. If we get a pint of berries this year it will be a miracle," observes Mrs. P. "We haven't had any rain in ages. Already what little grass we have is dormant like August. That does not make for good blueberry weather."

They are walking along the road, Putz on the blacktop, because he is nursing a sprained ankle. Mrs. P is in the firebreak.

Not a hundred yards from their driveway, P stops and says to his bride, "Look! A young bear."

"Oh!" she replies.

"I wonder where Mama is?" P asks out loud. "It's only a year-old cub. Normally, ma and kid hang together for two years."

"Oh!" says Mrs. P again, a little louder, as she moves from the firebreak to the blacktop.

Putz raises his camera to capture the image, but as he presses the release button he finds he had not advanced the film. Naturally, while he does this, the little gal/fella is off into the woods on the other side of the road. No shot.

Mama bear never shows.

Along their two-mile hike they hear sandhill cranes and see a deer in its summer red coat, standing in a grove of pines.

Later in the day, fishing in the lake, they spot a mature bald eagle sitting in the top of a tall tree on the edge of the lake. They have heard that a pair of eagles has successfully nested this year and wonder where the nest might be. Later they watch the eagle soar over the lake looking for fish.

Still later, they find the nest—built near the top of an old white pine on a small island.

"They sure build them big," comments the ever-observant Mrs. P.

"They add to the nest each year. There is one along Highway 60, near the Wisconsin River, that is over eight feet tall. Next year this pair will add to this nest, presuming they return, and someday, if continuously used and the weather doesn't do it in, it too will be humongous," added Putz.

"Am I going to get a lecture every time I make a statement?"

"Not a lecture, just adding commentary. If it is news to you, so be it. We should always try to learn something new every day. I am just helping you."

He paused. There was no reply, so he added, "It's all part of retirement, dear."

Throughout the day they watched a pileated woodpecker

pop up and down and flit from tree to tree looking for something to eat; a mother merganser with six very young ones scurrying across the top of the water following her; and four Canada goose families, totaling 30 individuals.

A great blue heron, a couple of mallards, and three solo "bachelor" geese rounded out the trip. (Oh, yeah, they did manage, between the wildlife watching, to catch enough fish—a rock bass, two bluegills, a pumpkinseed, and four yellow perch—to make a meal.)

When they got back, P's sister stopped by and while the women were talking, a big hen turkey strode in front of the window. A few minutes later the hen returned running and then flew across the river.

"Apparently, she has not made friends with my three golden retrievers yet," says P's sister.

Putzer had headed for the grill. He cooked up a dinner of long-baked sweet onions sprinkled with dill weed, blackened baked potatoes, burgundy mushrooms, and venison sirloins.

"An appropriate meal for a special event," stated P to his spouse.

They toasted the day with a sunset by the pier, while the onions and potatoes were filling the air with good smells.

A hot bath and fire in the fireplace ended the day again.

"Well," asks P to his wife, "do you think you will be able to adjust to retirement?"

"Retirement? When was I ever working?"

"Oh, you must be tired to give me an opening like that. I'll leave it go."

"Thanks. I must admit this was not a bad way to begin my new life, retired."

Five minutes later she was asleep on the couch.

Until we meet in, on, or near the river,

Keep a good thought!

The Peshtigo Putzer

One Rainy Day

Outdoor experiences come in many ways. Here Putz has "experienced" two days of labor outdoors, and now is "forced" to rest. He does, but continues to experience the outdoors. Today, in ways he otherwise could not do.

It had been an uneventful trip into Wishigan Country. Uneventful that is until Putzer began unloading the landscape timbers he had purchased from the top of his truck.

Actually, he noticed the problem before he took the timbers off; it, the problem, made itself known when he wanted to open the rear window of the truck cap, so he could lower the tailgate to unload the immediately needed items. The window would not open. It was pinched tight. The racks on the top of the cap were bent. The entire aluminum top had sagged to the point where the cap window was jammed tight. That was when the trip became eventful.

He had purchased magnum-sized landscape logs back home because they were on sale. He loaded them at the supply depot, then hauled them north. It was cheaper than purchasing them locally. However, it now appeared as if it may not have been a bargain after all. One hundred and sixty miles of highway driving had taken a toll—maybe a permanent one.

Fortunately, as Putz removed each timber, the bend in the topper became less. As the last one was removed, the window appeared to be back to level.

"I have always said I'd rather be lucky than good," P said to no one, because there was no one else around. This was a solo trip.

The trip was designed to replace the steps leading down to the pier. They had, over the years, become decayed, slippery, and sagged in places at a most dangerous angle. At least this was the opinion of Mrs. P. (And we all know, Mrs. P is NEVER wrong.)

It took two days of good, hard, design-as-you-go work, to compete the project. It went well. Of course, P did not have anyone there to tell him how to do anything, nor to alter or interrupt his work schedule, so that helped. The fact that he did not fish at all probably had something to do with the speedy way in which the job had gotten done also. (He did swim three times a day. It was a dirty, hot job, and the river was always a very welcome break.)

When P awoke on the third day, it was raining. A hard, straight down, no wind, downpour. The view from the window was as if one were looking out at the world from under a waterfall. (There are no gutters on the cottage.)

"My, my," Putzer said to himself. "Looks like a day of rest. I can do that."

After breakfast, the rain let up a little, settling into an all day soak.

"This is good for the land, and the steps will get a good washing and filling in of the cracks," he mused.

Putz settled into the chair in front of the window and picked up the latest edition of one of his favorite magazines.

This publication is not your everyday outdoor slick. This is P's "escape/dream" bi-monthly. Through it he learns of guns, art, and fishing equipment he will never own. He goes to places he will never see. Even if he should get six good numbers someday, that prize would have to be in double digit millions to be able to afford what these ads and articles display. Still, it is one of his favorites.

P "reads" this periodical in the same way each issue. He goes directly to the last page for a column entitled "Quotes." He reads these first.

These are, usually, true nuggets from a wide assortment of well-known outdoor scribes, many of whom are no longer with us, except for their words. All quotes are submitted by the readers, and then said submissions are further winnowed by the magazine's editors.

After "Quotes," he goes to the cover and begins to page through the entire magazine, looking at the titles, photos, and ads. He reads almost nothing at this time.

This page-through completed, he returns to the beginning and reads it from front to back. Many times all of the stories and columns are completely consumed. Only rarely is an article skimmed over. Never is one completely passed by.

Today, as the rain continued to fall, and by the time P had gotten through with the initial reconnaissance, he had napped twice.

Two ads impressed him: The first is a full page spread with an inviting young lady (one must keep the circa in focus) sitting in a boat holding a shotgun, with the words "A Classic Sweet 16," an ad for Ithaca Gun. On the very next page is an ad which declares: "How sweet it is."—from Kent Cartridge America—for their shotgun shells. Coincidence, or good planning on the part of the design editor?

As he began reading, he found that Sotheby's auction set several records: $684,500 for a Canada goose decoy carved by Elmer Crowell, and the identical amount of money for an 1866 Winchester carbine.

Later, he read more about lever action rifles, and the Lucas McCain influence; a fourteen-year-old pointer named Cindy, who loved to hunt woodcock; how one writer got "hooked" on bass, and how a couple for the grill is not a bad thing; one place to go if you want to catch silver salmon on flies until your arms drop off—Putz made a note of the flies; what it takes to hunt Dall sheep in the mountains of Alaska.

There was a reprint of a story by Ernest (Papa) Hemingway.

On and on—guns, pheasants, decoy makers, and, of course, sporting and wildlife art.

By the time P finished reading, he had napped four or six times (he didn't keep count) and the rain had stopped.

There was a hint of a promised sunset and he noticed it was almost supper time. He had missed lunch. No matter.

He poured his favored libation and walked down the newly-laid steps, nodding his head in approval as he went, to the pier.

"Very nice, if I do say so myself." Again to himself.

From the pier, he looked up river. A crack was showing in the cloud line. There would be a sunset. He toasted the day.

Tomorrow, Mrs. P would arrive. The final judgment on the steps would be made. He was not worried.

He toasted again.

Until we meet in, on, or near the river,

Keep a good thought!

The Peshtigo Putzer

Skeletons

We all have skeletons in our closets. There are no exceptions. Some bones rattle louder than others, but everyone has a flawed frame hidden somewhere. Putzer is no exception.

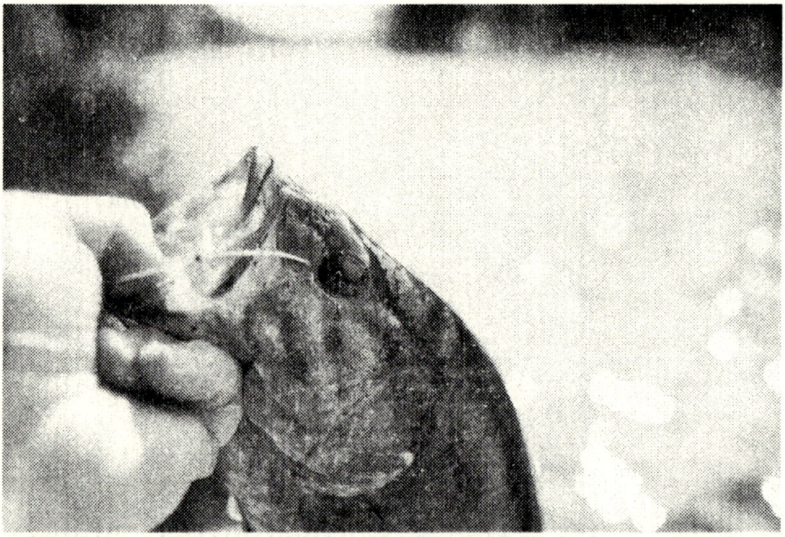

It was sometime in his mid-twenties. He is not certain of the exact year, and I was not his scribe at the time, but it had to be after the wedding, which was his twenty-first year, and because it happened in Wishigan Country on the river, and he was with his dad; therefore, the second cottage had to have already been built. Yes, it had to have happened when he was 25 or 26—still young, easily influenced, intimidated, and respectful of his elders.

It was an extended weekend. The family had come up Thursday night.

Friday morning, early, Putz sneaked off on his own and went trout fishing. He caught his usual small fish, but he didn't mind nor get discouraged, because even though fly fishing was not exactly new to him, trout were different than bluegills and crappies. The flies were sometimes similar, but the approach was different, and the entire mental state of mind was different.

Trout were difficult. Everyone knew that! Everyone wrote about how to catch trout. How it took much time and patience to catch trout on flies. It wasn't like dunking a nightcrawler and leaving it lying on the bottom of a hole until something, be it trout or sucker or chub, came along and slurped it up, taking the hook with it. No, he could not be discouraged. This was the ultimate in the fishing world, as it was known then (early 1960's).

So he came home happy, but still... a good-sized fish caught on a fly would have really been nice.

Putzer had his chores to do at his in-law's cottage and his dad had his to do at his own place next door. Once in a while, they would give each other a hand when the work load required it, but during the day, they pretty much did their own thing.

As the day wore on, everyone went for an afternoon swim, then had an early supper, scheduled to accommodate the fishermen.

After supper Putzer and his dad went fly fishing for panfish. Bluegills and crappies were in the shallows, looking for favorable places to make their beds, fool around a bit, and propagate the species.

It was a little early in the day for poppers, Putzer's favorite way to take these little scrappers, so Putz began with the fly already tied to the end of his leader, a Coachman wet fly, the last fly he had fished with in the morning. Dad manned the motor and P handled the oars, as any good son would do.

They both fished and often had two 'gills on at one time. (A double hook up, something I believe the TV shows get all excited about today.) It was a great evening just drifting and casting, catching a fish now and then. The fishing was good, and so was the catching—there is a difference; they are not the same.

To the west, clouds were building, looking like they might bring rain before the evening turned to night.

They continued to float.

The sky darkened and the water got smooth as glass. Putzer switched to a yellow popper. Even though it was still a little early, the conditions were right. He cast to some fallen tree tops, let the popper settle... then twitched it. Pop! The bug disappeared. A big orange-bellied bluegill pulled and tugged and went round and round at the end of the line. Putzer landed the fish. When it was in the boat, they both stared.

"Wow! A dozen of these and we'll have ourselves a feast," Putzer's dad said. Putz agreed. The fish was indeed a keeper, nine inches long and an inch across the back.

A light rain began to fall.

"Think we ought to head home?" Putz asked.

"Not if the fish keep biting," replied his dad.

They continued to cast to the brush and continued to catch the big bulls. Eventually, the spot petered out, or the fish moved on because of all the commotion.

They continued downriver, the rain falling a bit harder.

On the corner just before the lake, Putz cast to a patch of lily pads. A small bass, perhaps 12 inches, took the fly and a short fight ended in the boat. Putzer released the fish.

"Why did you do that?" asked his dad.

"The season doesn't open until tomorrow."

"Oh."

Another cast, another small bass, another release. Putzer placed the next cast closer to a log that lay on the edge of the pads. The fly disappeared in a larger-than-life dimple of rain as the drops got bigger. Then the sky really opened up and the rain came down as if poured from a bucket.

"Let's head home," said Dad, cranking up the motor.

"Not just yet," said Putz. "I'm snagged on that log."

Then the snag moved. The fish bored deep. The fly rod bent double. Dad shut off the motor and reached for the net. Putz brought the fish close to the boat and Dad made a pass with the net. It was a smallmouth bass. A very nice smallmouth bass—estimated weight, three and a half pounds. The good-sized fish Putzer had hoped for earlier in the day.

The rain was pouring. No one else was on the river. Dad took one look at Putzer and said, "You throw that fish overboard and you will follow it." He cranked up the motor and they returned home.

Now, the question is: After showing the prize to everyone the next morning, (it was too wet to display it that night, so they stashed it in the live box) did they release the fish? After all, it was caught out of season, but the season was now open.

Only God and the fish and a few close friends know for sure.

Admittedly, this skeleton rattles softly, but it is still a skeleton. What about you? Is there a skeleton in your closet?

Until we meet in, on, or near the river,

Keep a good thought!

The Peshtigo Putzer

Sometimes You Need a Good Belt!

"We should try to learn a little something new every day." This Putzer believes, and tries to adhere to. Some days that is easier to accomplish than others. On this particular day, he learns something new alright. However, as is his style, he does it the hard way.

The truck humped and bumped along on the back road, winding its way to the river. He didn't hurry. There was plenty of time. A buck, in velvet, looked up, then disappeared with a single leap into the plush green summer forest as the vehicle poked its red hood around the bend.

"Nice to see you," Putzer said to the whitetail, "Hang around a few more months, finish developing those horns, and let's do lunch sometime in October or November."

He pulled the Chevy into the familiar grassy parking area, turned off the ignition, and just sat a while looking at the river and listening to the sound of the water pushing its way through the descending old rock that shapes the class III whitewater rapids.

The sun was about an hour away from dropping behind the hill that rose sharply on the opposite bank of the Peshtigo. That would give him about two, maybe two and a half hours of fly time. Perfect.

"Looks like it will be a good evening," he said to himself.

Getting out of the truck, Putz strolled over to the base of the rapids. The river was at summer norm. Wading would be just the way he liked it. He could work his way up the right side, short lining the pockets as he went. Then he would come back down to the center, and begin crossing, again wading upstream, being careful of "The Big Hole."

Finally, as the sky darkened to dusk, he would work a few more of the backwash eddies and deep pools on the left. When he ran out of whitewater, he would walk the shore and cross at the riffle, some 100 yards downstream.

Back at the truck, he put his fly rod together, strung a 6X leader to the loop at the end of his line, pulled on his waders, checked the vest pockets for the fly boxes with the patterns he would need, and removed those he wouldn't.

When satisfied, P slipped the vest on, and placed his hat on his head. He paused. He looked at the wader belt with the net attached, and decided, "I won't need that tonight. I don't feel like cleaning fish."

It didn't appear that there was any action on the surface right now, so P pulled out and attached a #12 brown Rapids Nymph, a fly of his own design that had served him well in this stretch of water for more than twenty years.

Pocket poking his way upstream, he picked up a few small rainbows. Nothing spectacular, but fun on the little two-weight rod for sure.

The sun sank behind the hill.

At the top of the rapids, he switched to a Royal Coachman, size 14. "Let's do a little prospecting," he thought. "I see a few dimples here and there. Let's find out what's making them."

He caught four chubs.

Walking back toward the center of the fast water, Putzer paused at the water's edge and switched to a #10 black Bivisable. "If you're going to fish 'em fast and late, you better give them something both they and you can see." So was his philosophy.

Feeling his way past and through the boulders for about ten yards, he began his systematic casting of the fluffy fly—hitting the eddies behind the larger rocks and letting the fly dance down the little shoots on either side.

As with the first trek, his casts were short. Sometimes no more than the length of the leader plus one foot of line. Always he worked toward the opposite shore and up. Eventually, he would end up at the top of the rapids again. At least that was the plan.

About a half hour into this second leg of his fishing plan, Putzer hooked into a really good fish. It caught him unawares and got below him before he knew it. This fish had lived here a long time; it knew every rock and obstacle in the entire rapids and it was willing to use all of them if necessary. Putzer could not let it do that.

The trout made a run from the little pool it had been feeding in, broke from it, and literally leaped downstream until it found another pool more to its liking.

In the process Putzer had to give line, and a considerable amount of slack got between him and the fish. That was all the fish needed.

The new pool had a log wedged on the bottom and the trout took that slack line and wrapped the leader around the log—as trout will do. It all happened much faster than it takes to tell.

The fish was gone. Putzer was standing with a tight line, but it was tight to a log.

He started to walk down to the hole to free the hookup. He had just placed his right foot on the top of a rock, and was lifting his left, when the rock shifted (or did that trout push it?) and Putzer fell backwards.

Here's the picture: A full grown man clad in chest-high waders, holding a fly rod in his left hand; his feet are in the air, and he is being pushed downstream in whitewater and heading, fortunately feet first, for one heck of a ride through the class III whitewater if he can't right himself, and so far, he can't. It is almost dark, ***AND**, his boots are filling with water*—because he did not put on his belt, because he decided not to use a net.

Do you have any idea what this scenario is like? It ain't fun. It's scary.

The current pushed him toward a collection of fallen trees and large rocks. If he could just grab hold of the first log, instead of getting sucked under it, he should be able to pull himself up and out—if he could lift all the water that now filled his waders and was making him ride very low in the water.

Of course, he accomplished just that (how else could this story be told?), but how it happened without breaking his rod he doesn't know, because if the truth be known, he didn't think too much about the rod when the time came to grab the log. (By the way, the fine leader that was wrapped around the log by the trout that started all this, broke off almost immediately, which probably saved the rod from breaking.)

As he pulled himself up, some of the water spilled out. That was good. He kept prone and edged his way along the log to the big flat rock. He was lying on his stomach, so most of the water ran out—slowly. When it became practical to stand, he did. He leaned the rod against a tree, took off his vest, and struggled out of his waders.

There wasn't a dry spot on him, except his hat.

Fortunately, the current had brought him to the same side of the river where he had begun this sortie. He would not have to walk the woods and cross the riffle.

Picking up his rod, he reeled in the limp line. Then he lifted the vest and boots and made his way, in stocking feet and dripping clothes, to the road and back to the truck where he stripped down.

As some may know, P keeps a well-supplied vehicle for just such occasions, so he had a towel to dry himself and dry clothes, including underwear, socks, and shoes, to change into.

The drive home was enjoyable. It wasn't cold. The stars were shining, and the people population was low.

Putzer always tries to learn something every day. This day, and forever after, what Putzer learned was that when he wades he will always wear a belt—whether he uses a net or not.

And don't you forget it!

Until we meet in, on, or near the river,

Keep a good thought!

The Peshtigo Putzer

Some Days Are like That

We know that not all of Putzer's misadventures involve fishing and hunting. But who would ever think that a casual trip to the local landfill would convince P's grandchildren that he was... well, you'll see what I mean.

It was not a bad day.

Oh sure, he dropped his paddle this morning when the bass hit his popper just as he was setting the rod down with one hand and picking up the paddle with the other. So, he got a little excited. Nothing lost—except the fish—but... it's not the first time, and it certainly won't be the last.

Anyway, he got the paddle back. That's why he always

carries a spare. It didn't float too far while he attempted to horse the Smallie into the net. It would have all worked out too, but he didn't know the net had a hole in it. Must have gotten snagged somewhere.

The rest of the morning went okay. Breakfast was good. Putzer liked his toast and bacon a little on the dark side with hard fried eggs—occasionally. Well, they didn't go to waste. He can't help it if he gets distracted with the shenanigans of the birds and squirrels that flit and scamper around the cottage. Heck, that's one of the things he likes about the place.

The yard got cut and trimmed (by Mrs. P). Hadn't he loaded the trailer and truck and taken it, with the grandkids, to the landfill? The kids wanted to go, remember. They begged. It wasn't his fault that they will never trust him, or ride with him, when he goes to the dump again.

You be the judge.

As I said, after breakfast, Putzer spent a good hour loading the back of the truck, and then the trailer, with a lot of stuff. Mostly, years of accumulated junk, that even he had to admit, he couldn't find a legitimate reason to keep any longer. It was tough, but it had to be done.

As he was about to leave, the grandkids asked if they could go along. He said it would be okay, but they had to realize that it might be as long as two hours before they got back. Could they sit that long and behave themselves?

Both moms agreed it would be a great experience. Actually, they wanted the break, and two hours of no kids sounded just fine to them.

"Take your time," they shouted. "If you are good, Grampa will stop and get you an ice cream cone on the way back." (That should be good for at least an extra five to twenty minutes, they thought.)

The trip, "to the dump," the MAR-OCO LANDFILL, was

uneventful. They watched the road sides flow past, played word games, like, "I spy something...," and generally were good kids. That ice cream was already looking good to Putzer; the day was getting quite warm.

When Putz and the kids got to the landfill, they weighed in and were directed along the roadway to the fill area. They got to where Putzer normally dropped off the junk, but today he was directed further into the fill, across the top of recently-deposited garbage, covered with only a token amount of sand.

"Where are we going now Grampa?" asked Kate, the older of the two passengers.

"See that big truck over there, we have to go next to it."

"I don't want to go there. It doesn't look nice over there," stated Zach, the second traveler. "And this place stinks!"

It should be explained that it was near 90 degrees by now. Ever been in a non-air conditioned truck with the windows open, on top of a pile of garbage? Not exactly the beach. It should also be noted that Putzer's truck is not four-wheel drive.

"It won't take long," Putzer assured the duo. "We'll be on our way in no time. Then we'll get that ice cream and go for a swim."

Putzer crept forward across the spongy desert.

The kids became very quiet... sat very still.

Putzer parked the truck and trailer along side of the semi. The driver was in the process of emptying what looked like coal dust. Turns out that is what it was. He was dumping the power company ashes.

"Looks like you are pretty deep with those wheels," Putzer said to the driver.

"Yeah. I'm stuck. They are trying to get the big cat in here so they can get a cable on me and either pull or winch me out. They really should have added more topping to this pile before they sent us driving on it. A couple of people have had to get helped out today."

Putzer glanced at his own tires and started to unload double time.

As he got back into the truck, and was about to pull away, a garbage truck pulled in on his left—close. Real close.

He could not go forward. He could not swing to either side. He had to back out.

Now Putzer has problems backing up trailers, especially this one, because it has a very short tongue. That, plus the soft, rutted, spongy terrain. Well, the trailer jackknifed as if that was the only thing it wanted to do. It didn't move one inch back.

Putzer looked at his passengers. He was about to say that they would have to sit there awhile until the garbage truck moved out, but the two kids were staring straight ahead, holding each other with both hands, and very slowly and softly repeating these words: "We are never going to see our mothers and fathers again. We are never going to see our mothers and fathers again. We are..."

Putzer got out of the truck, looked at the situation with resolve and determination. He got back into the truck, pulled ahead, just a bit, then cranked the steering wheel as tight as it would go and backed up, twisting the trailer back until it touched the rear bumper. The next inch would have bent the trailer tongue.

"We are never going to see...," the words droned on.

Twisting the steering wheel to the max the other way, he pulled forward, and, with an inch and a half to spare, cleared the garbage truck, and drove out of the heat, the flies, the sand, the smell, and the garbage.

It wasn't until they had stopped at the gate, paid the fee, and were on the regular blacktop that the kids stopped their chant. (The last couple of times they did say it with smiles on their faces.)

The ice cream was truly enjoyed and when they got back to the cottage, and their moms, the tale was told over and over again.

Upon questioning, it became apparent that the kids were serious. They thought their grandfather, he who could do many marvelous things, had betrayed them. They were going to die and be buried right there in the dump, and Grampa Putzer was to blame.

Needless to say, they didn't think that for very long, and all was forgiven and the whole incident was laughed at numerous times, but the next day, just for fun, Putzer said at the breakfast table, "I didn't have room for everything yesterday, so I have to go back to the dump this morning. Want to go along?"

"No way, Jose!" they replied in unison.

Now, I have to ask, why? Why wouldn't they go with Putzer? It wasn't his fault.

Anyway, they decided to let the second trip to the dump go until another time and talked Grampa into taking them fishing instead. Which, of course, he did.

Until we meet in, on, or near the river,

Keep a good thought!

The Peshtigo Putzer

In the Good Ol' Summertime

Most people have summer as their favorite season of the year. Most, but not Putzer... EXCEPT for one activity. There is something, something not normally spoken about or admitted to, that P really loves to do, and it can only be done in summer.

Summertime and the living is easy." So go the words from the Gershwin classic opera, *"Porgy and Bess."*

Putzer hates summer. Well… *hate* is a pretty strong word. He doesn't *hate* anything, but of the four seasons, it is safe to say that summer is his least favorite. He can always get warm in spring, fall, and winter by changing and/or adding clothes, but he can take off just so much before he gets into trouble, and often times, after he is barely (pun intended) legal, he is still uncomfortable.

There is only one thing about summer that is really special. Oh, he likes shorts and bare feet and the late evening fly fishing opportunities, but when the temperature gets above 80 and the humidity is the same, there is only one activity he looks forward to that does not produce sweat and discomfort. And when he does it, he must admit, he does enjoy it to the fullest.

He doesn't remember the first time he tried it. I'm sure it was with some trepidation. After all, it wasn't as if everyone was doing it. Surely he wasn't the first, but it was his first time doing it because he wanted to. And he really wanted to!

He remembers it was definitely one of those hot, humid nights. He's not sure which month, probably August. The drive north hadn't been too bad, but now that everything was unpacked and the cottage on the Peshtigo was "open," he was sweaty and sticky, very uncomfortable. He needed relief.

He stood on the pier, his ice-filled Manhattan glass dripping with sweat. For a Friday night, it was pretty quiet. The moon, a little beyond its last quarter, was already high in the sky. It looked a lot like the old Miller moon, but without the girl.

He set down the glass, walked slowly to the end… and dove. Relief came quickly. First, it was the tips of his fingers, then the whole hand; then his arm and head almost simultaneously; his shoulders and neck came next; then his chest and back; down past his buttocks and legs; and finally, the very tips of his toes cooled a little, as he sliced into, and was engulfed by, the river.

It wasn't that the water was cold; it was that his body was so *hot* that the water felt cold. Actually, the water was warm. "Bath water," he called it, but it was cooler than the air. There was relief.

He swam to the center of the river, "hung" there a while, treading water; then swam back. Once next to the pier, he hesitated, looked around, then slipped out of his trunks and continued his cleansing swim.

It's called skinny-dipping.

According to my 1996 RANDOM HOUSE WEBSTER'S COLLEGE DICTIONARY, and ENCARTA 2000:

> skin'ny-dip', v., -dipped, -dip.ping, n. informal. -v.i. 1. to swim in the nude.

Simple, right? Well, yes, for most it may be just that, but for Putzer, it is more than a simple swim without a suit. It is a summer ritual, rite, ceremony. After a half a dozen or so, autumn can come any time.

As I said, skinny-dipping is the one thing about summer that Putzer really looks forward to.

Now, let me qualify that.

Skinny dipping in natural water, not a pool, is what Putzer really looks forward to in summer.

Natural water, lakes and rivers, have a different feel to them than a pool. They have a coolness, even when the water is warm. Rivers are better than lakes, because rivers have currents.

In summer the currents keep the water cleaner than water that only moves when the wind blows, or a boat makes waves.

Currents make a difference.

To stand with your feet on the bed of a stream, on sand or gravel or perhaps on a large rock, and feel the water moving over and around every part of your body is very relaxing. This is not at all like the pulsing pounding one gets in a whirlpool or hot tub. This is a natural flow. Nature's massage.

You become an object in the path of a natural force. That force builds up against your body on the upstream side, and applies a slight pressure before it passes to the right and left brushing your sides, then swirls back to you, in the form of a gentle eddy, on your downriver side. You are a rock. If you stand there long enough, fish will take up residence.

Putzer will "dip" whenever he gets the chance—even in broad daylight—when the place is right.

There is such a place, or six, in Wishigan Country. It is a rarely traveled portion of a stream. It has a clean, firm, sandy bottom with four "deep pools" behind Precambrian granite that ended up at various spots in this stream just so Putz can enjoy an afternoon in the sun without too much worry about being "seen."

Here the current is always strong. Putz can swim against it and never move if he adjusts his stroke to the force of the day. If he keeps his pace a bit under that of the current, he can actually paddle forward and end up going backwards—fun.

When moving from pool to pool, he sometimes is only knee deep or less in water, allowing the sun to warm and the breeze to dry the skin between each deep water dip and frolic.

Earlier, I mentioned this spot is rarely "traversed." That is important, especially to Mrs. P. She is a bit more cautious than P, but, as he says, "Heck, that just adds a little seasoning to the adventures of daytime dipping. Nobody's going to see anything new or different that they haven't seen before. And it's not like they are going to be within arms reach of us if they do come by." At least that's his philosophy. Mrs. P *does not* share that point of view.

One of the things people don't like about dipping is that body parts that are normally covered are now exposed to the *wild things* in the water.

"Nonsense," says Putzer, "You don't go dipping in water that you wouldn't swim in anyway. That is common sense. Gracious! What do you think is going to happen? Think a musky going to nip at your… toe? Not likely."

Anyway, it is "Summertime…" and the dippin' is easy.

Until we meet in, on, or near the river,

Keep a good thought!

The Peshtigo Putzer

An August Potpourri

It is no coincidence that this tale follows the previous one. The early words enforce what was said in detail in the previous tome. Other than that, it is just another day(s) in the life of a true putzer and his noble companion.

They left for Wishigan Country on Sunday, around noon. Normally a three hour drive, they arrived at the cottage at 7:30. They had gone by way of Clintonville to have a look at a trailer, then weaved their way east and north through country they hadn't seen for years.

The trailer was a bust, but viewing different territory at a leisurely pace was a treat.

By the time they unloaded and got settled in, it was deep, deep dusk.

There had been a lot of dust during the drive, coupled with the near 100% humidity. They did not hesitate slipping into their swim suits... then into the river... then out of their suits for a cooling, cleansing swim—the only good reason for August!

The next morning Mrs. P went for a walk while Putzer launched both the canoe and the boat, then looked to the project of the trip—replacing the sides of the pump house.

The original structure was built about ten years ago from old barn boards, which Putz had purchased some twenty, twenty-five years ago from their "egg lady" for $15. The family had removed one side of her barn, then stored the boards in the garage attic.

The original plan had been to use the wood for paneling, but that never happened. With the exception of making a few picture frames, the only other project the wood had been used for was to build the pump house. The majority of the side of the barn still was protected from the weather in the Putzer garage. Because it only took ten years for the old wood to completely rot, Putz decided to replace the sides with treated plywood, and to just trim it with barn wood strips for aesthetics.

"No one will notice the difference once the plywood grays," Putz assured Mrs. P, who had some reservations about the looks of the plywood.

The project took most of the day. A day filled with digging sand, sawing and hauling and hammering in 85 degree-plus, humid weather. The river felt *sooooo* good after the work was done—even with a suit on. (After all it was only 4:30 in the afternoon, not the recommended time of day for skinny-dipping with all the boats on parade.)

After a supper of grilled chicken, baked potatoes, and salad, the Ps went fishing.

The river traffic was still heavy, so they took the boat and headed for the lake.

At the point where the river flows into the flowage, they found a lady stranded in a BIG pontoon boat. The motor had died, she was alone and anchored. The boat was too big for the Putzers' 14-foot fishing boat, with the mighty 9.9 outboard, to pull.

As they were discussing the predicament, along came another pontoon boat—four guys and a girl who had been fishing all day. One of the guys offered the distressed lady the use of his cell phone if she could get to their boat. The Putzers shuttled her.

After making the call, the lady stayed on the deck of the smaller pontoon boat. They made a very cheerful group as they roped the stranded vessel to theirs and chugged off into the lake, heading for some destination pre-arranged via the cell phone. They had indeed made the best of a potentially poor situation.

"I do believe they are actually enjoying the entire event," said Putzer.

"It certainly sounds that way," agreed Mrs. P, as the laughter and boats faded in the distance.

The Ps began fishing, but the fish were off feed.

In the morning, Putz took the canoe and drifted downriver, fly casting as he went. He only got about a half-mile, when a strong wind came up and began blowing him toward the lake. Coupled with the current, Putz could foresee a definite problem returning, so he reversed his course and paddled his way, trolling a streamer, back to the pier.

The good news is that the wind brought in a "cold" front with lighter, less humid air—sunny and lowering the temperatures to the mid 70's.

The Putzers decided it would be a good day to explore, so they headed for trout country—Carney Rapids. Mrs. P learned a bit more about wading in chest-highs and the joys of sitting in the middle of a small stream with her legs dangling and water rushing around her feet. She determined that even in the boots, "... fast water is *cool*—in more ways than one."

The fish were still not cooperative, Putz catching only one brookie on a nymph.

They returned to the cottage and went for their swim before

supper, then fished downriver after the dishes were left to air dry in the rack.

Until now, they figured the wildlife, as well as the fish, had taken the week off—only one hummer (hummingbird) had come to the feeder. With all the driving and boating they had done, they had only two sightings, although they were pretty neat.

They had drifted up to a snapping turtle with a 16-inch shell—it made quite a wake when it finally submerged—and there had been a quick glimpse of a coyote on the way to Carney.

Tonight, however, things picked up a tad. While drifting toward the lake, they heard a whippoorwill, and heard and saw four sandhill cranes. Then, as they were motoring home and the sun was disappearing, a woodcock zigzagged across the river.

It was 46 degrees at 6:45 a.m. when Putz paddled upriver. Life continued to improve. The coolness roused the wildlife and fish a little from their summer doldrums. Putz caught a couple of nice smallmouths on a white Wiggle Bug, cast and trolled among the rocks, and he had the company of an otter family and a great blue heron.

Of course, this all made sense because the Ps had to leave, so, naturally, everything was going to improve.

After putting the boat and canoe away, they cleaned the cottage, packed the truck, then took what might very well be the last swim of the season. It would be a month before they could return, and the water just might be a tad cool by then—maybe, maybe not. (It wasn't.)

On the way back to their normal year-round home, they talked about looking forward to the B&B they had reserved for their bike trip in Minnesota. (And yes, they do venture beyond Wishigan borders from time to time, but then, don't we all?)

Until we meet in, on, or near the river,

Keep a good thought!

The Peshtigo Putzer

The Story of "Two Bear"

Putzer has not always been a putzer, therefore not always called "Putzer." There have been times in his life when he "earned" other names. This is one of those times, one of the names, and how he earned it.

Long, long ago, in a galaxy not very far away... in a country called *Wishigan*, there roamed a young man called "Two Bear."

(Isn't that a neat name— *"Two Bear"*? The name conjures visions of a great Native American, a chief of the mighty Ojibway tribe. [God, I hate having to be politically correct at a time like this. "Indian" is a much stronger and visually beautiful word— "... a great Indian chief..." —but... what can I say?] This chief would have been known as, *"Nenij Nabek."* Too bad the name didn't stick, but I suppose it wouldn't be as appropriate today as it was then.)

It was his father-in-law who dubbed him "Two Bear." Mrs. P never picked up on it, but his in-laws did; and continued to use the name until they passed on to the happy hunting grounds, where I wouldn't be surprised if they were referring to him that way yet today.

How did Two Bear get his name?

Well, I would guess that he must have slain two bear, right? Well, like the fella in the Hertz, Rent-A-Car, TV ad says, "Not exactly."

Fifty some years ago, even before Ms. M became Mrs. P, in their courting days, Putzer was an avid bow hunter. Not very good yet, but he really liked the sport.

There were no compound bows in those days. Actually, P shot a bear, Grizzly, reflex bow—a forerunner to the recurve. (Now, I know that goes back a bit, but it was several years after the chariots had been replaced by automobiles.)

One Saturday afternoon in late September, Putz, his future bride, and her father, (who was not about to leave those two in the woods alone together even if it was hunting season and they were about to be married in two weeks) went to a spot they referred to as "The Oaks"—a local name for a forty or two, north of Benson Lake Road, near Goodman Park.

The plan was for Putz and his lady to take a stand along a runway while P's father-in-law-to-be made a little circle drive in an effort to move a deer or two in the youngsters' direction, and perhaps put a venison tenderloin on the grill that night. F-I-L-2-B would carry his trusty Savage 12 gauge pump, in hopes of finding a "partridge" (Ruffed Grouse) or two.

That was the plan.

The "little drive" took about an hour and a half, maybe two hours. Nothing moved, or if it did, it didn't move in Putzer's direction. Not only that, but the woods remained silent—not a shot had been fired.

The "hunt" over, the three participants were walking single file along an old established deer trail on their way back to their vehicle. The path was hilly. Nothing big or deep, but occasionally the last in line would lose track of the person ahead of him—particularly if that person dawdled (or putzed, if you will). Not a problem, you understand, but you have to know this to realize the full impact of the situation when it happens.

The scenario is this: Father-in-law-to-be is in the lead, followed, six or eight steps behind by daughter, with Putzer bringing up the rear. (Although he was never thought of as Putzer at the time, he was developing the proper habits and traits, even then at a ripe young age.)

Putz was poking around, looking here and there, his mind on tracks at this particular moment. When he came to the top of a ridge, he almost knocked his future wife flat on her keister, and her dad along with her.

The future Mrs. P's father had his gun to his shoulder, while she was almost hugging his backside. Putzer figured a grouse had just flushed, but couldn't figure the anxiety of his intended. Then he heard his future dad say, "I wish I had a slug!"

Putzer looked to where the 12 gauge was pointing, and there stood two black bear—a yearling, maybe 150-200 pounds, and a very big sow—at least four ax handles wide across her backside.

(Now for those of you who do not remember, or never have known, there was a time in Wisconsin history when bear hunting was legal during the deer bow season, and special permits were not required.)

Putzer looked at the situation and very quickly, much faster than it takes to tell, made the following calculations and decisions: "If I shoot the little fella, he will scream and mama will not be a happy bear. If I shoot mama, it better be a good shot because we don't want a wounded black bear on our hands. I can shoot, have a powerful enough bow, the arrows are capable, but there are two other people here with me, granted one of them has a shotgun, which is quite adequate at close range, but do we want to have to deal with "close range?" I don't think I'm that good of a shot. Don't they look pretty? Never have seen two together like this before. What a neat sight. There they go."

Very few words were spoken during the rest of the hike back to the vehicle, or on the trip home—just a little mumbling. Something about, "... chance of a lifetime... never get another opportunity... nothing to worry about..." You get the idea.

And so it was, that from that time forward, whenever he was summoned by his father-in-law, it came out "Two Bear."

I don't have any proof, but it is my understanding that two weeks later, at the church, there was some effort made to have the preacher ask the groom, "Two Bear, do you take this woman...etc.," but it never happened.

Today, he answers to many names, "Putzer," among them. He outgrew the, "Two Bear," and the "chief" look and style.

"Putzer" has become much more appropriate, and continues to fit his style. *"Nenij Nabek"*? I don't think so.

Until we meet in, on, or near the river,

Keep a good thought!

The Peshtigo Putzer

Can One Grouse Really Make a Season?

There was a time when a successful season of grouse hunting meant cleaning a lot of birds. But times change, and so have Putzer's perspectives.

The paper said it should be a good year. The cycle was up. The woods were full of Ruffed Grouse. "And hunters," Putzer thought out loud, barely audible, to himself, as he read Dave Otto's column in the "Press-Gazette."

"If I remember correctly, the last time the cycle was up I

ended up with one bird. Too darn many hunters in the woods. Tell them (hunters) the birds have rebounded and every Tom, Dick, and Mary comes ridin' the back roads lookin' for *partridge*. Why can't they just hunt pheasants or ducks? Heck, after the first week, the birds have seen so many blaze orange vests and caps, they think it's deer season. I honestly think they turn nocturnal just like the deer do. Why..."

"What are you grousing about?" interrupts Mrs. P, knowing full well what he was saying, and tossing in the intentional pun.

"Oh, nothing earth-shaking. I'm going for a walk. Alone, if you don't mind. While I still can." And off he goes, putzing his way down along the river bank into the alder thickets, the 20 gauge side by side cradled in his arm, wearing his *brown* hunting vest and *camo* hat.

He did it not so much for the hunting, it was really a bit early in the season and still too warm for his liking, but rather as a form of making a statement. (Even if there was no one around to see or hear it.)

Tomorrow was Friday, and the local population of *homo saps* would indeed grow for the weekend. In spite of them, he was saying he could still find a spot or two without running into another hunter—at least during the week.

Well, the weekend came and went, and so did the hunters. Putzer was right, of course, there were more hunters in the woods and driving the roads now that there were birds to chase.

As the season progressed, much to his surprise, Putz hunted with more different people than he ever had done before, and with a kennel full of new dogs.

You may remember, the Putzers don't own a dog. They used to, but...well, that's another story.

Anyway, P enjoys watching a good dog work. Contrarily, he does not look forward to a day in the woods where the dog hunts in one county while the hunters hunt in another. This particular year, because he hunted with a wider variety of people and dogs, it seemed there were more times when he only saw the dog at the beginning of the hunt and again at the end. Consequently, there were grouse seen (from afar) and heard, but very little shooting—by anyone.

Eventually, he got back to hunting with Mrs. P. They would venture forth on their own, at their own pace, enjoying the day for what it was, directed only by whatever part of Wishigan Country they wanted to see, with the length of the day dictated more by the weather than anything else. During the last week of their season, before shutting down for the winter, they flushed more than thirty birds. Most were pretty edgy, and of those thirty, Putz only had four shots. His pattern covered one bird.

Now, for many, one bird would never be considered a good season. And for a time it even disturbed P. That is until he reflected back on it.

The night before they were going to leave for home, he sat before the fire remembering.

Some of the trips were truly total disasters both dog- and bird-wise, BUT...Putz still had good times with his friends. He saw some new territory, which is always enjoyed; had some great field lunches, and added a few photos to his file. Simply put, they (the hunts) were, if not always productive, fun.

The paper was right, the birds were abundant. However, it just so happened, more often than once, that when the dog of the day did work properly and a bird did get up, in range, in front of the dog, the dog was in front of its owner, so naturally, the owner, and not P, got the shooting. That's fair, of course, and was no reason for Putz to be upset, which he wasn't, but the fact was, he did not have a lot of shooting opportunities—which really means, opportunities to say, "Oh darn, I shot behind again."

At the end of his thoughts, as the fire died, he said to Mrs. P, who was reading, "You know it was a pretty good grouse season after all. Not so much in numbers bagged, perhaps," he continued before she could reply, "but in birds seen and the quality of the hunt."

"Quality?" she said, lowering her book and looking at him in her best matter-of-fact-stare. "I thought you hated all the crowds that filled the woods. And what about the times when you spent most of the day looking for the dog instead of the birds? You enjoyed that?"

"Well, no, I did not like the crowds...and a day or two were not the most enjoyable because of canine difficulties," P replied, "but you know, I hunted with old friends and met some new people through other friends. I did get to see some good dog work. You know I always like being out with AJ."

"You only hunted with AJ once," her voice becoming a bit more forceful and rising a decibel or two. "You just admitted that most of the time you had to hunt for the dogs more than for the birds. I really don't understand."

"Yeah, yeah. But *we* did put up a bunch of them feathered critters."

"Yes, and if it hadn't have been for the one that flew into our door and broke his neck, to add to the one you did finally hit, we wouldn't even have a complete meal for the two of us. You call *that* a good season?"

"Well...yeah. I guess it's all a matter of one's perspective."

Until we meet in, on, or near the river,

Keep a good thought!

The Peshtigo Putzer

His Biggest Catch of the Year

Shortly after this incident, Putzer became an advocate for barbless hooks.

The original plan for the second week in November 1999, was to do some final grouse hunting, begin bow hunting, and *if* the weather cooperated, and got up to near 50 degrees, give the muskies a final fling.

That was the plan, but here it was, November 9th and the temperature in Wishigan Country was near, and possibly above, 70 degrees. Too windy for grouse, and too hot and dry for deer hunting. It was not a day for the woods. It was a day to be on the water. Putzer went fishing.

He trailered the boat and headed for Caldron Falls. At least his plan for one last try for the mighty muskellunge would be in order, even if the balance of the week wasn't going as planned.

(Actually, what he really *needed* to do was run the carburetor dry on the old 9.9 Evinrude. He forgot to do that earlier in October. Once that was done, he could tuck the whole outfit—boat, motor, and trailer—away for the winter, a season that would get here one of these days, but not this week, according to the weatherman from Channel 5.)

Normally, Mrs. P would be with him, but her schedule called for other activities, so this would be a solo day.

After launching at Landing 13, he motored out of the bay planning to begin fishing the rocks and island in the middle of the lake. Once outside of the bay, however, it was breezier than he thought. The main body of water had waves that were only an inch away from whitecaping. He could never hold a boat at the rocks, so Putz motored directly across to the weed bed on the other side. (Why is it the best fishing is always on the other side of the lake?)

"So, my day might be a bit shorter than planned, by eliminating one spot," he mused to himself. "No never mind. Just so I remember to run the engine dry."

Putzer began tossing a modest-sized plug instead of the normal monster muskie lures. He figured he'd give northern pike an opportunity to join in on the fun as well. He wasn't proud. Heck, this was a bonus day for him, why not for the fish? How many times in November can they, the northerns and muskies, get involved in a friendly tug of war?

Two and a half hours and three weed beds later, P headed back toward the landing. The wind had picked up, creating that previously missing inch of height required to turn the tops of some of the waves white. He would fish the bay leading to the landing; it would be protected.

Putzer switched to an old jointed Pikie Minnow, and cast to a fallen tree. After the retrieve he cast again, this time placing the antique lure inside the confines of the branches.

P tugged a bit on the line. It appeared as if the plug would pull out if he just applied a bit more snap and pressure. Putz did. It did. And quicker than it can be told, Putzer had a hook in his arm.

Now Putzer believes in keeping his hooks sharp. He never fishes with store-bought-hooks-fresh-from-the-box until he has hand-sharpened, gently and meticulously, each hook on his baits. It was one of these carefully-honed hooks that was deeply buried in his arm, beyond the barb. He had indeed sharpened the hook to perfection. There wasn't even any pain.

There Putzer sat. A large wooden plug dangling from his right forearm. This would never do. He reached with his left hand for the trusty *Leatherman*, (not a commercial) and cut the hook from the plug. Now he could move around without fear of doing any additional damage. He figured it was time to go home.

Putz started the motor, remembering to run on only the gas in the carburetor, trailered the craft, and drove home.

Once home, Putz consulted with his neighbor, a nurse by trade. Her first question was, "When did you last have a tetanus shot?"

"I don't know," was his answer.

"Then I think you'd better go into town and have this removed by the doctor so you can get a shot too. I could probably pull it but I don't feel comfortable doing so without knowing about the shot."

So Putz drove into town, had the hook removed, and got the tetanus shot. The doc had to use a special tool, which was inserted from behind the barb, to shield the barb, while he pushed the hook around and through. The shield was needed because the barb was hanging up even though it was being pushed forward. There must have been a rough edge somewhere. (Maybe Putzer hadn't done such a good job sharpening that hook after all.) The doctor also prescribed antibiotics.

Looking back at the entire situation, Mr. P was a pretty lucky guy. When he reenacted the event, he realized that if his arm had not been positioned as it was, that hook would have ended up in his neck. That would not have been good. Also, if he had continued to try and remove the hook by himself, (he did try) who knows what kind of trouble he might have gotten himself into.

The nurse had done a lot of sterilizing of the area on the arm, and then the doc "numbed it," so there was no pain and therefore no unpredictable moves and reactions to the pushing and pulling during removal.

The lessons Putz learned are simple: Hooks do get stuck into more than just fish or other people, and it just might be better to go over to release the plug from the hang-up, rather than trying to *jerk* it off. (*The jerk* could be at the working end of the line.) And, if you must pull that lure out of a tree, cover your face and neck. It is easy to have hooks removed from a forearm.

Until we meet in, on, or near the river,

Keep a good thought!

The Peshtigo Putzer

One Day on the River

There are those who might contend that when one tries to do too much at one time, or in one day, one cannot do anything well or correctly, thereby accomplishing nothing. That depends on how you define the word "accomplish." (Or if you even care.) But, don't take my word for it, ask Putzer.

Putzer *loves* October, *but*, there are so many things to do, and just not enough time to do them all.

One thing he does make a point of doing every October is a one-day float trip, downriver from their pier. It is a day he hunts and fishes and photographs and enjoys to its fullest. It is a day of restful rejuvenation.

Let's take a look and see what one of those days might be like.

Ideally, weather-wise, it is sunny, with puffy white cumulus here and there; a slight breeze, preferably from the south, southwest; temperature 40 in the morning, 50 to 55 in the afternoon. There is color on the shore. The current is not strong, just steady.

No one goes with P on this day. He does this alone.

After breakfast, Putz loads the 17 foot Grumman double-ender: One camera with three lenses. Binoculars. One large thermos of water, a smaller one with tea. A banana, two cookies, red licorice, and a sandwich. One gun, a .22/.410 over-under, equipped with a peep sight. An antique casting rod and reel. (Which means he has owned both since the late 40's. Some things are hard for P to give up. Hey! They work. He is used to using them. Don't knock it.) A small tackle box with all the old reliable plugs and spoons and some Junebug spinners, bell sinkers, and three-way swivels. Nightcrawlers, a net, one anchor, a raincoat just in case, (to cover the camera) two paddles, and a cane pole, round out the required items to make it a complete day.

The gun is loaded, set for the .22 barrel, leaning against the thwart in front of him. (For those not familiar with Putz's weapon, the .22 is the top barrel and the .410 the lower. The gun has an exposed hammer, and within the hammer is the barrel selector. It is a real fun gun.)

P pushes off from the pier. The current takes hold of the canoe and only an occasional touch with the paddle keeps it on a predetermined course. This first section of river always has big grey squirrels prancing and scurrying around.

Putz finds one sunning on the branch of a poplar.

Setting the canoe paddle across the thwart and reaching for the over/under is done in one motion. The gun comes to the shoulder. P is able to float to within ten yards of the dozing bushytail, and puts the peep sight on the gray's head. Ping! And the grey falls from his perch into the Peshtigo River.

He sets down the gun, picks up the paddle, then nets the squirrel.

About a mile downriver P beaches the canoe and switches the selector to the .410 barrel. It is time to see if he can find a grouse or "Timberdoodle" (woodcock, to the uninformed).

After an hour, hour and a half, through a mixed terrain of tag alder, oak, and poplar, while traipsing along a small creek and its sloughs, Putz flushes one grouse, unseen but heard, and two wood ducks. The Woodies would have offered shooting if he had been carrying a larger gauge gun with steel shot.

"They will be there tomorrow morning," Putz notes to himself.

It's time for lunch.

There is a deep hole below a group of huge Precambrian rock structures in the middle of the river. Normally, it is difficult, (read impossible) at best to fish, because of boat traffic. However, this being the middle of the week, there is no one here but P.

He anchors, rigs the rod up with a ten foot section of ten pound mono. A three-way swivel is attached to the mono. From the lower swivel, he drops a modestly heavy bell sinker from a 12-inch, four pound leader, and on the remaining swivel he strings three feet of six pound mono, to which he ties a Junebug spinner with a #4 hook. On this hook he impales a large, squiggly nightcrawler.

Putz lowers the rig into the depths, just on the other side of the rocks, allowing the current to take everything slightly downriver.

The resident eagle makes a pass overhead, and dips a wing to say, "Hi!" It, too, is "doing lunch."

Putz says to the eagle, "Hopefully, there is a walleye or two who is also hungry."

Putz begins to eat his sandwich.

He has a few taps and/or nudges as he munches, but nothing he can put a hook into. So be it.

Lunch finished, P pulls the rig, switches the rig back to its casting mode, and attaches a number 4 Mepps bucktail. He then pulls the anchor and continues his float.

At a small island, he again beaches the canoe. This time he pulls out the camera. A small cove across the way just must be shot (photographed)—golden tamaracks reflected within a patch of green and yellow, with an occasional, slightly red-edged lily pad mixed in for good measure.

It's time to head back. P snaps on a floating, jointed Pikie minnow—the old wooden variety—picks up the blade and begins a slow, bank following, paddle upstream.

He stops at a stump, dropping half a nightcrawler from the cane pole. A "pumpkinseed" is raised from the depths. A bit small, it goes back.

Along the edge of a weed bed, a pair of northern pike find the old Pikie to their liking. They go on the stringer.

Along about three-quarters of the way back to the cottage, Putz stops in a little inlet to check out an old logging road.

A woodcock startles him as he almost steps on it when he gets out of the canoe. A bit later, he finds another bushytail, romping in the oaks. He also finds grouse but can't seem to find the range, even though two give him opportunities.

As he returns to the canoe, and his trip back to the cottage, it is late evening. The wind has died. The water a mirror.

"If this were August, I'd be casting a surface plug for bass. What the heck, why not?" he says to himself.

He snaps on another old friend, an Injured Minnow—perch finish.

A cast here. Another there. Then troll it behind as he heads home.

Wham! Mr. Smallmouth hits that trailing tantalizer like he hadn't eaten for a week. It too goes on the stringer.

Back home. Putz puts the three fish into the live box so he can pose them tomorrow. (It is too late for photos without a flash, and P doesn't like flash fish photos.)

It has been just the kind of day he had hoped it would be—some hits and some misses.

Putzer's October day on the river.

Until we meet in, on, or near the river,

Keep a good thought!

The Peshtigo Putzer

Putzer Learns about Tree Stands

Tree stands have been popular for a long time, but P has never taken to them. Then, as this story unfolds, he is offered the use of one that, maybe, is worth giving a try. So he did. Did the experience convert him?

It's the first week of November, and, even for Wisconsin, it's cold! The thermometer on the cabin window reads eight degrees, an hour before dawn.

It climbed to a whopping twenty-three by one o'clock in the afternoon, or so he was told. Don't ask him, he's been in the woods all day. Presently, he is frozen stiff on a little platform, leaning against a tree. He is about to lower himself back to terra firma and head home. It has been a long, and totally different day for him, and he has enjoyed every minute of it.

Obviously, the old boy is deer hunting. Bowhunting, to be precise, and he has just experienced something he has never done before—he has spent the majority of the day in a tree stand. Who says you can't teach old dogs, or putzers, new tricks?

Tree stands have been a legal way to hunt deer for a long time, but some people never adapted. Putzer is one who has never taken to, "...one of those blinds-in-the-air."

Oh, he tried.

Over the years, he tested a few of the "permanent" ones—those platforms made of scrap lumber supported by tree limbs and 2x4's that are reached by cockeyed 1x4's held to the tree trunk by eight-penny nails—but their permanency has always been suspect to him.

Of course, there are more substantial ones, those playhouses on stilts, complete with heaters and satellite TV. (Heck, he heard that one was so big and plush that the "hunter's" wife held a "Grand Opening" cocktail party in it for all of her friends. True story.)

And these little portable platforms people carry on their backs and clamp around the trunk of a tree ten, fifteen, twenty feet in the air, and sit or stand on? No thank you. Not for him!

In other words, for Putzer, deer hunting means keeping his feet on the ground—period.

So why is he up a tree, and how did he get there?

Actually, it happened quite by accident.

Putzer's "stand" is a 30x40 piece of plywood, leaning against an oak, supported by 2x4's seven feet off the ground, with a 2x4 ladder. There is a small seat, balanced on a three-quarter-inch pipe, bolted to the top of the platform. But it is a few bolts shy of steady, so he decides not use it.

Instead, he sits on the edge of the platform with his feet on the steps. He is still not comfortable. The whole set up tilts forward, and the wood is covered with old crystallized snow. He keeps slipping forward.

He gets down. Looks around. And makes a few adjustments with some wood scraps found at the base. He is able to jack the ladder up enough to make the platform level, even give it a little tilt backwards.

The stand belongs to his nephew, located on the family's land. The nephew suggested he use it, saying there were bucks in the area, and he should give it a shot—literally.

Putz figures, "What the heck, it's a reasonable size and only five steps away from Mother Earth. I can spend a couple hours at it. I always have the option of going elsewhere."

The nephew showed him the stand last night, so he could find his way in the early morning pre-dawn. Which he did.

So there he sits—waiting. His feet off the ground.

After two hours he gets antsy. This is another reason he doesn't use tree stands. He likes to move about—shuffle...still hunt...putz.

This is the first time he has hunted this eighty. It is very defined—high line to the east, roads south and west and a recently logged area to the north. He takes the tour.

There is still enough snow from two days ago to leave good sign and there are a lot of deer in the area. He finds a couple of places where he can return later if his nephew's stand proves to be more than he can handle.

After an hour of scouting he works his way back to, "My platform in the sky," as he thinks of it, and readies himself for a few more hours of wildlife watching. He has always been told that one sees so much more with your feet off the ground...maybe.

It's about 10:30 a.m. by the time he settles back in—the best he can.

He hunts with a 54-pound, 62-inch, Bruin Custom Recurve

and shoots instinctively. He practices from all practical positions, so shooting while sitting is not abnormal for him, except for one fact—he usually has the ground to shift around on, or drop a knee to.

From his "perch," he tries different angles, and finds he can cover everything pretty well, just as long as he remembers not to drop to his right knee as he rotates to his left—a natural move for him.

He has a problem with the openness of this kind of hunting. His only cover is a small oak right out front—he can see over the top of it, but it blocks out about twenty yards of shooting lane. Otherwise he is just sitting there. Out in the open, like a mermaid on a rock, for all to see. He is used to cover all around, to hide his movements.

He finally gets settled, when the first buck of the day comes into view. (Yes, the first!)

The buck has spikes about six inches long and he's approximately forty yards out. He is moving from Putzer's left to right on a trail which will bring him within thirty to thirty-five yards.

The buck never sees him, or if he does, Putzer doesn't seem to bother him any.

Putz watches the young buck, waiting for an opening. The young buck ambles off the trail and begins feeding on acorns, in the opposite direction.

Thirty minutes later, a nice six-pointer comes slowly down a trail that will walk him right up Putzer's ladder into his lap, if the buck stays on it. This buck too is feeding on acorns and sniffing for doe at a leisurely pace.

The only problem is that little clump of scrub oak directly in front of Putzer. For a clear shot he will have to wait for the buck to pass under the left side the oak. Then he will be in an opening ten yards in front of the stand.

"Don't kneel," Putzer whispers inwardly.

While still behind the protection of the oak, the buck's nose turns him on to a crossing trail. Putzer never gets a clear shot. The buck never knew Putzer was there.

He, Putzer, is impressed. "Maybe this off the ground stuff is as good as everyone says it is," he thinks to himself.

Believe it or not, a third buck approaches shortly thereafter, to Putzer's right.

This buck has one spike about six, maybe, eight inches long and one small fork. When he is thirty yards away, Putzer draws and releases. The tip of the bow hits the edge of the ladder with a click! The buck jumps as the arrow speeds right to where he had been.

That ends the shooting for the day, but another little "spiker" walks through, again using the trail of the first one. He looks right at Putzer, and stares, his little shiny two/three inch spikes glistening in the only splash of sun that breaks through all day.

Putzer stays on that 30x40 piece of plywood for the remainder of the day. Total count—fifteen deer, many of which would not have even offered a shot with a rifle, but he did see them, and some he knows he would not have seen if he were in a ground blind at the base of the tree instead of seven feet above.

The highest activity times were around the middle of the day, when those four bucks passed through, and during the last half hour of the day. How many of the other deer were bucks? Possibly an additional two to the previously mention four, but he wouldn't bet the farm on it.

So does this mean that Putzer is now going out to buy himself a tree stand and join the thousands who stand vigil on these teeny weeny wedges of metal with their safety belts and special equipment to keep themselves comfortable and/or prevent nose diving to the ground if they doze a bit?

Noooo!

Will he build his own stands? Maybe.

But he would want them big enough to allow for a tripod and other camera equipment, because any of the bucks that passed his way, and several of the does, would have been sure "hits" with his camera and short telephoto, if he had had enough room for the equipment in addition to the hunting gear. He thinks that might become excessive in size. (Of course, Mrs. P could always use it for entertaining.)

We'll see. He has to give the entire day a bit more thought. Certainly, it was a great way to see wildlife, apparently unnoticed, or at least in less disturbing postures than when keeping both feet firmly on the ground...yes, it has merit.

But right now, he is cold! His thinking on this matter will have to wait. Right now he's headed for a hot bath so he can thaw out. (One's blood does not circulate very much when one just sits in a tree all day.)

And so it was that Putzer learned about tree stands—sorta, kinda, maybe.

Until we meet in, on, or near the river,

Keep a good thought!

The Peshtigo Putzer

How to Get a Deer to Come in Really Close

Want to learn Putz's secret of how to get a deer to come in really close? Read on.

It is Friday night. Not just any Friday night, but THE FRIDAY NIGHT. The Friday night before ***The Opening of Deer Season***. Tomorrow morning, an hour before sunrise, Putzer and all the gang in camp will be out on their stands—looking, searching, waiting for that elusive critter known as a whitetail buck.

"Remember, no does. Not 'til later in the week. Not 'til we still have tags to fill and someone wants venison to eat. Don't go shoot'n no doe unless you haven't found a nice tender buck. You want meat in the freezer, and this is your last day to hunt." That was the camp rule.

It was a carryover from the old days when the deer herd was limited and does were not even legal. (Remember? If you do, you have a few hunts under your belt—as does Putzer.) Sometimes P thinks that is why he is so reluctant, even today, to shoot antlerless deer, and why he hardly ever fills a tag—maybe, just maybe, that is the reason.

No matter for this tale.

This particular Friday, Putzer traveled to the old log cabin by himself. He could only stay for a day and a half. He had other commitments for Sunday night that he could not get out of, so, because everyone else would be leaving later in the week, he drove solo.

The trip went well, except, of course, for the traffic, but that was expected. The day would come when he would eliminate that part of the season. The weather cooperated and the roads were safe. He could see that there had been a fair amount of snow, but the plows had done their job.

When he came to the turn off into the "driveway," a mile of old logging road through the woods to get to the cabin, it was very evident that the days before had been full of that wonderful white stuff—there was a foot of it in the woods. Fortunately, the other members in camp had blazed a trail.

As beautiful as it was, and as much as Putzer loved snow, he drove very cautiously. There are many hills and curves that make the trip in, during the daylight hours, interesting; at night, when the headlights leave the track and shine only on the trees ahead, but you know the road drops down and turns to the left, it can be a downright scary challenge.

Coasting down the final hill and seeing the lights in the cabin was a welcome sight.

Putzer parked his truck, picked up a pack and headed for the door. He stomped off the snow from his feet and walked into the warm room. Tom and Jim were at the table playing cribbage, while Bob tended the fire and read a book. P's father-in-law was cooking something for tomorrow. The whole place glowed and smelled just right.

"Well, look what the cat dragged in. Howdy P! How was the trip? Need a hand unloading?"

"Nah, I'll get everything," replied Putzer. "You guys look too comfortable. Besides, I don't have that much. Only be here tomorrow and half of Sunday."

After Putz got settled in, there was the standard talk about how and where everyone would hunt in the morning. Putzer decided that, because O'l Man Winter had come a little early to Wishigan Country this year, and the river was already frozen over, he was going to deviate from his usual stand at the crossing, and explore the opposite side—to see where the deer were coming from and perhaps why.

It is not often that he could hunt across the river without going to the trouble of hauling the old wooden skiff in and out of the garage. That wasn't real bad, but if he did shoot his buck, the trip back could get a bit tricky—the skiff was not exactly large or steady.

He'd pack a lunch and spend the day. Although he said he doubted if he would really need the lunch, because, "I should have my buck hanging by noon."

Right!!

And so it was that on Saturday morning Putz walked out of the cabin door, strapped on his snowshoes, hefted the borrowed .32 caliber Winchester Special, Model 94, and ventured forth into a part of the woods he hadn't seen for several years.

The land across the river from the cabin starts with a hill, a big hill. Putzer worked his way slowly to the top with the aid of a flashlight. There he paused and decided to sit awhile and watch the little flat on the other side of the "mountain" until the light increased and he could get his bearings.

It would have been nice if I could tell you that the sun came up bright and clear and warm with little wind, but that would not be true. There was no sunrise. The woods turned from black to dark grey and eventually a lighter grey. The clouds hung low and looked like they were filling up with moisture. There was no wind.

"Not a bad morning," Putzer mused. "Now let's try to sit a while longer and let the woods forget you are here, and see if something worthwhile wanders by."

It should be noted here that Putzer is not a sitter. He likes to think of himself as a "still hunter." The truth be known, however, he does some of his best *putzing* in the woods. He moves here, shuffles there, sits awhile, follows a promising looking track, watches the squirrels and mice and chickadees. In other words, he putz...well you know.

Noon came and went and Putz hadn't seen hide nor hair of a deer. He ate lunch on a stump overlooking a small spring-fed stream, which still had a little open water here and there, feeding the Peshtigo downstream from the cabin.

"That must be the Rat," Putzer thought. "I guess I better think about heading back. Didn't realize I'd gone this far."

As he turned to head back, a light snow began to fall. He was happy for the "webs." Plowing through a foot and more of snow is no fun without snowshoes.

About three p.m., Putzer found himself below the cabin along the river at the familiar crossing.

"I think I'll find myself a good stump and sit the rest of the day. I must have traveled five miles today—closer to a hundred the way I feel," Putzer confessed to himself.

He found a low-cut stump conveniently located with a good sized tree for a backrest, overlooking the trail. He slipped out of the 'shoes.' The snow had stopped and the clouds were breaking up.

"It will get really cold tonight," he thought to himself as he wiggled into a bit more comfortable position.

It didn't take long and Putzer's eyes closed and his head slowly slipped down.

The next thing he knew, his gun was sliding. He grabbed it unconsciously, and only then realized he had "snoozed a bit." He peered forward, and lo and behold, there, directly in front of him, in the fresh snow, were tracks...fresh tracks...*very fresh tracks*. Deer tracks. He traced them with his eyes.

The tracks came from the opposite side of the hill. Seeing Putz, the deer hesitated. Because there was no movement, it continued forward and advanced right up to Putzer's feet. He could visualize the deer smelling the odd looking "stump," and, deciding it was nothing of interest, or to worry about, it moved off down the hill, crossing the river where many others, for many years, had done before.

This was the only deer Putzer had "seen" all day.

"Oh well," he consoled himself. "It was just a little deer anyway. Probably just a doe."

Until we meet in, on, or near the river,

Keep a good thought!

The Peshtigo Putzer

The Turning Point

All good things come to an end. Sometimes, if we are lucky, that end becomes the beginning of a new legacy—but not always. Take, for instance, the gun deer season of 1969, the year Putzer took the biggest deer of his life.

It was in 1969, which marked the end of the way one man did things and how, in a way, another's began. Allow me to explain.

For several years, prior to '69, Putzer had joined his father-in-law for opening weekend at "the old deer camp." TODC was the kind of camp stories are written about and dreams are made of—a log cabin, a mile from the blacktop, a power plant for electricity, situated on the banks of the Peshtigo River. The cabin was two rooms, one big kitchen and living room with a fieldstone fireplace, plus the bunkhouse that slept ten—cozily.

The members of the camp would also fit into any legendary tale—they had hunted together for years, always stayed the entire week. There was a cook who ruled, and everyone else did the dishes and any other chore that needed doing.

The food and drink would never be found on any of today's "good for you" lists. It was simple, hot, and well made—just plain good—ham, pork hocks and sauerkraut, turkey with all the trimmings on the proper day, oxtail soup, and all the sausage, cheese, raw onions, and amber liquid a man could handle.

But in '69 the TODC was gone—not physically—the cabin remained, but most of the members had died off and the remaining couldn't hunt anymore, physically. All but one. Putzer's father-in-law remained.

Because he was not about to do deer camp alone, he, P's father-in-law, decided he would still hunt deer, but from his own place. It wouldn't be the same, but he would at least be hunting.

The plan was for P's father-in-law and his wife to go to what would someday become the Putzer cottage for the entire deer season, with P and Mrs. P and their family coming up to spend Thanksgiving. Putz would hunt Thanksgiving morning, Friday, and half of Saturday. Then everyone would pitch in to shut the place down, so by Saturday evening they could all return home without the holiday traffic. The cottage season would then be over until spring.

When the Ps arrived, they discovered that Mrs. P's father had really not hunted much.

"I don't know," he said, "it's not the same any more. You go out and hunt. I'm done."

There was snow on Thanksgiving morning north of Fox Hill along Parkway Road. Putz sat and mooched (putzed) in familiar sections of that area for a few hours, but saw nothing.

Friday was much the same. He spent the day hunting around the old camp...just because, well, that's where he had always hunted.

He was using a borrowed .30-06, topped with a variable powered 4 to 7 scope. He wasn't really comfortable with the weapon, but his other option was the old .20 gauge, full choked, bolt action, J.C. Higgins that never checked out too good at the range.

As the day went on, he wished he was carrying the Higgins. A scope gets in the way for a guy who is not a sitter. Even at a young age, Putzer putzed. Especially when he went deer hunting.

"Still hunting," is the proper name for what he did. To still hunt properly and comfortably, one needs a short, lightweight gun. The Winchester 94 would have worked great, but it was not his, and even though it was not being used at the time, he felt he should not ask, just in case there was a change of heart from his father-in-law.

P saw several doe on Friday, but not having a "party permit," bucks were the only legal targets he had. (Remember, this was 1969, not today.)

Saturday Putz decided to hunt in new territory, nearer home. There was an old road that led up to the Caldron Falls dam. It was Public Service land and open to hunting. Looking for grouse earlier in the year showed lots of deer sign, but it was heavily hunted opening weekend. Perhaps this late in the season no one else would be there.

He parked the station wagon at the old bridge and, in the predawn light, walked toward the dam. He found a comfortable stump overlooking a valley that led to the river.

"This would be a proper place for a man with a scope-mounted cannon," he mused to himself. Then he settled in to wait.

There was less snow here. In fact, the slopes facing the south were void of the white stuff.

The sun came up in a clear sky. It wasn't cold, maybe 25

degrees. As the sun rose so did the temperature; by noon it would be 50. A good day to end the cottage season.

Putzer sat for two and a half hours, then he shouldered the gun and began to ease his way back to the car. He walked slow and careful, stopping every fifty feet or so. You never know what might be around the next corner or behind the next tree. He was about halfway back when he paused and scanned the woods on each side of the road.

If the buck would have just stayed down, he would have been alright. Putz would have never seen him. But, of course, that is one of the reasons a still hunter is successful. By pausing and standing for ten or more minutes in one spot, the game thinks it has been seen, gets nervous, and moves, giving the hunter an opportunity.

The buck stood up and stared at Putz, standing broadside.

Putz slowly raised the rife. He looked through the scope and saw only brown. He hadn't a clue what part of the deer he was looking at. Looking with both eyes, concentrating with the one off the scope, he put the brown filled scope-eye where it appeared the shoulder was and squeezed the trigger. The scope almost broke his glasses when the gun recoiled.

The buck leaped once and was gone.

"So much for scopes," Putzer said to himself. "Still, I don't think I missed."

He went cautiously over to where the deer had stood. It had been bedded down at the edge of the hill that rose from the river, giving it a great view of all below. The road Putzer was on was on the same level as the bed. Evidently, the brush gave the buck the required security from that side.

The hill was long and steep. Putz scanned the bottom along the river bank. Nothing. Then, as he continued his search, he saw him—halfway down the hill, literally draped around a tree. He had to be dead. No self-respecting animal would be in that position on purpose.

P approached carefully. Touched the eye with the barrel and

slipped on a small patch of snow, sending him tumbling headlong toward the brush and rocks on the edge of the river. Fortunately, he was able to stop himself before hitting the water.

"Getting this fella home is going to be fun!" he thought. "I hope I can keep the buck from sliding down like I just did. We'll both end up wet."

Before cleaning out the buck, Putz tied its head to a nearby poplar. Now he could work without worrying about the carcass sliding. The gutting was easy; gravity pulled everything out of the cavity.

The climb to the road, however, took some doing. Drag uphill twenty feet, rest. Drag, rest. Heart pounding, even at that young age. More than once P lost his footing when that buck stuck his antler or foot around a small bush or tuft of grass, but the deer never got away.

At the station wagon Putz loaded the body onto the tailgate. The car sagged and groaned. Putz was puffing and sweating. He was dirty, but he had brought home the bacon, so to speak.

Back at the cottage, there was a small celebration and they hung the carcass to cool.

The deer was eight points and weighed 165 pounds dressed. It would have been nice if it had been shot around the old cabin, as a fitting tribute, but it wasn't.

"Maybe," Putzer thought to himself, "some other day—maybe not."

Until we meet in, on, or near the river,
Keep a good thought!

The Peshtigo Putzer

Post note: Time will record that Putzer's father-in-law did try again to deer hunt the next year, but, as in '69, for him, a way of deer hunting had died. He had tried a new way, but it wasn't the same. It would be up to young P to carry on, if he so chose. To make the decision final, P's father-in-law presented Putz with the Model 94. Putz still has it and it still shoots straight.

Let the Lessons Begin

Sometimes the outdoors comes to us when we least expect it. Here Putzer gets the opportunity to teach a little fly tying during the annual Christmas cookie baking weekend.

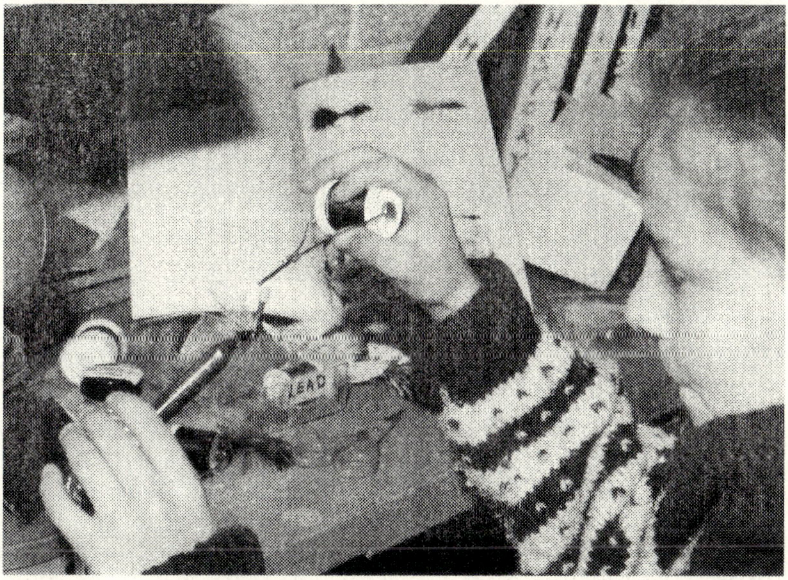

It is December 4, 1999. The Annual Cookie Baking Weekend in the Putzer household. All of the regular participants are there: Grandma Putzer (Mrs. P), Great-grandma Putzer (Putzer's 90-plus year old mother), Mrs. H (another 90-plus member), one of the junior members of the Putzer clan (CP), and a fourth generation Putzer (KP). Each year, the first weekend in December, all five females (occasionally there are two more) gather for the entire weekend, to bake and decorate Christmas cookies.

It is a tradition that goes back decades. Unfortunately, not every original member is still around, as some have passed on to the Great Cookie Kitchen in the sky, but fortunately the new and younger family members are beginning to fill the void.

(Nice, you say, but you are thinking, why talk about Christmas, and what does baking cookies have to do with anything in the outdoors? Just stay tuned. You will understand. Now, back to the story.)

Normally, in a situation like this, you would guess that here is a weekend when Putzer takes off and heads for the woods with his buddies, or solo, it doesn't make much difference to him, just so he is out of the house and not underfoot.

Au Contraire. Not so. You are wrong. Putzer is actually an intricate part of this weekend—he cooks the main meal and serves up the libations for the cocktail hour. He is also available to play gopher, and to take the youngest member of the tribe with him when she gets bored, to pick out and buy the Christmas tree and wreath. A good time for, I believe the popular word of the day is, *"bonding."*

(You know, I looked that word up in the dictionary with the intention of quoting how this "bonding" applies to the situation. There are 24 definitions to the word "bond," and none of them apply. Heck, Putzer and his grandkids don't "bond," they have fun and enjoy each other's company—most of the time. But I digress—once again.)

Anyway, Putzer is always involved with the big weekend, and for the most part, he enjoys it.

This, the aforementioned December, was no exception.

Everyone began arriving about 9, maybe 9:30 Saturday morning. An hour or so later, after a fresh pot of coffee and a donut or two, the mixing and baking began in earnest. The two ovens, one in the kitchen and the old one in the basement, were beginning to emit marvelous smells. The dining room was turned into the cooling and decorating parlor, with shallow dishes full of "jimmies" and "snowflake-like" candies, only an eighth of an inch in diameter, and "sugars." Each topping sporting all of the colors of the rainbow. As the day went on, the cookie crowns were replaced with egg whites and brushes, then powdered sugar. All in all, a very busy, and sometimes messy, place.

A couple of times Putzer had to "pick up a few things," and KP would go with him. The weather wasn't real good on Saturday, so they, P and KP, decided to hold off the tree and wreath buying until after church on Sunday.

Normally, Putz made the main meal on the grill so he wouldn't run into an oven conflict, but this year he wanted to make a Savory Pot Roast and that required the use of an oven for at least three hours.

"We can work that out as long as you use the oven in the basement," stated Mrs. P.

"No problem," replied Putz, "but I will also need the big bread board to use as a counter when cleaning and cutting the vegetables at the stationary tub."

That was agreeable, and about 1:30, P turned the laundry area into his kitchen.

While all this was going on KP, the fourth generation member of the group, was bouncing back and forth between decorating and cutting out cookies, "gophering" with Grandpa, and cranking up the old computer to play a few games.

After Putzer got all of his vegetables—the Wisconsin Russet potatoes, celery, carrots, onion, leek, and fennel—cleaned and ready, he browned the meat, added tomatoes and red wine vinegar, with the spices, and got the entrée baking in the oven. Now all he had to do was watch it for a few hours and keep things moist.

P went over to his fly tying bench and began to organize things a little. In the process he found that it would be a good idea if he replaced a few patterns that he lost over the past season.

Sitting down in the old wicker chair, he gathered the specific materials he needed to tie a yellow Woolly Worm, one of the patterns he needed to replace.

KP came over and asked, "Whatcha doin' Grampa?"

"I'm going to tie up some flies while supper is baking."

"Can I try?"

"Sure. Watch how I tie this one, and then we'll set you up and you can tie one."

"Great!"

Putzer finished off the fly, explaining the tools and materials as he recreated the attractor of bluegills and trout. When he was finished, he swung the vice around (P is left handed), handed a hook to K and said, "OK, your turn."

He showed her how to put the hook in the vice so it would not slip, handed her the bobbin of thread, and started her winding the thread over itself onto the hook, explaining the value of a short thread so the bobbin acts as a weight, holding the material in place, with a little tension, between each step of the process. As they tied this first fly together, Putz would again explain the materials and the parts of the fly—the tag, the body (chenille), the hackle, and the head. With each step, it became another yellow Woolly Worm.

When the fly was finished and the head had been cemented, K asked, "Can I tie another one...by myself?"

"I guess so. Here, let's move this one to the drying rack and you can begin again. Call if you need help. I have to get the girls their pre-dinner cocktails and check on the meat. It's beginning to smell like supper."

As Putzer went over to the oven, K began her second fly. This time she used different colors and other types of material that were scattered around the vice area. Putz would assist now and then when she had a problem, but over the next two hours KP tied six flies. All but the first were her own design, and many of them looked pretty darn good. (Of course, the fact that Putz had six of his fly boxes open next to her on the table may have had a little influence on K's designs.)

Upstairs the dining room table became just that, a dining table. Places set, the last draughts of the pre-dinner cocktails in hand, the group sat down as Putzer came up the stairs, supper in hand. He was followed proudly by KP. She was carrying the drying board with eight brightly colored flies on it.

"See what I have made," she beamed. (Putzer beamed a little himself, and everyone at the table noticed.)

Indeed, the lessons had begun.

Until we meet in, on, or near the river,

Keep a good thought!

The Peshtigo Putzer

Post Script: K since has continued to tie at least one fly whenever she has had the opportunity. Looks like Putzer is going to have to teach a ten year old how to cast those flies sometime in the next few months. Oh well...it's a dirty job, but someone has to do it! It just means that he will have to find more time to get on and in the water.

BOOK II

Tales of The Peshtigo Putzer

"Beyond Wishigan"

As stated in the Prologue/Conception, the Putzers do travel beyond Wishigan Country. And so, your question might be: "When this happens, is it possible that Putz and Mrs. P put on different personas?" Now why would they do that? Here are some samplings of what happens when they go "Beyond Wishigan."

—j.k.

Snow Trout

I know, this tale seems far-fetched, but it really did happen—at least the e-mails. Is it a little too bizarre? Well, you be the judge. After all, it is the opening yarn for our "Beyond" section.

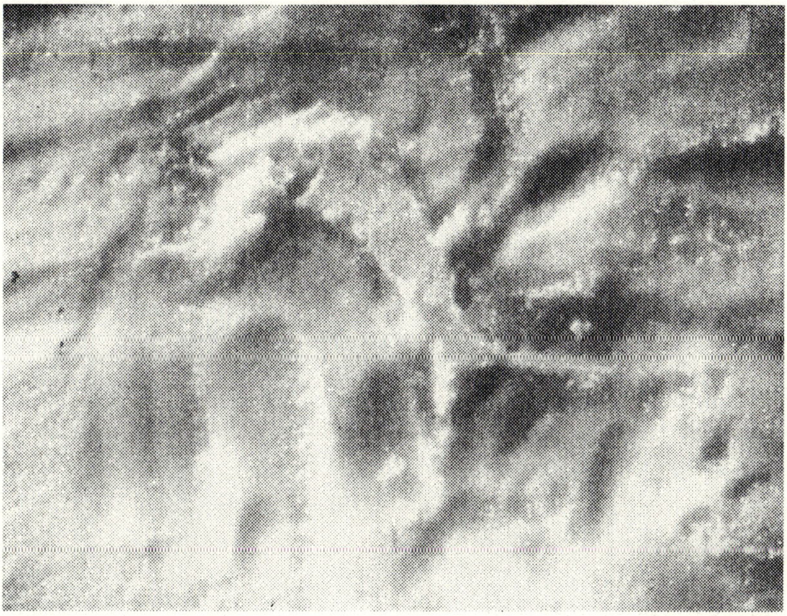

It began with a simple e-mail to one of Putzer's fly-fishing friends, Chris, one day in January.

There had finally been a little snow falling, which was welcomed by the Putzers, because they like to ski in January instead of fly fish. Not that P forgets about fly fishing; he does not. It is just that skiing makes more sense when it is 20 degrees with a foot of the white stuff blanketing everything and making things look bright and cheery instead of drab and brown.

It was because he does think of fly fishing in January that P e-mailed his friend in the first place. There was a travel/fly fishing seminar going on at one of the local fly shops and Putz wondered if Chris could get a night out and join him.

P didn't get an instant reply, but a day or two later when he did, it went like this: "Putzer, I'd love to join you, unfortunately I am working on a project that I have to complete or it will drive me nuts. You go and let me know if this is something we can really afford, or just another 'dream trip.' Talk to you later, gotta go before the snowflakes melt."

Now, normally, when Chris says he has to finish a project, Putz understands that to mean a project for work, but *snowflakes*?

Naturally, P sent a message flying back to Chris as fast as the modem would carry it. "What kind of project involves snowflakes?"

It took *five days* before P got an answer: "I am attempting to tie a fly pattern to capture, in order to photograph, a very rare species of Snow trout. A pattern that resembles a snowflake, which is what I believe the trout have been feeding on."

Naturally, Putz was somewhat skeptical, especially the rare species part of the message. Granted, they now had a little snow, and Snow trout do migrate with fresh snowfalls, but normally they prefer to stay in places where the snow hangs around for a while; otherwise they are continuously on the move and that gets to be tiring and can be dangerous if they get caught in a sudden thaw. Perhaps this was a subspecies of this rarely-seen breed that liked to travel more, and therefore has never been seen in this area before.

Putzer replied, "Tell me…tell me everything you can about this exceptional subspecies of Snow trout. Which subspecies is, was, it? You sure they weren't just a few white carp coming out of the river for a change of diet?"

Chris retorted, "Don't get smart. I know a trout when I see

one; besides, they do not have pink eyes. If you are interested, or if not, settle back and I'll tell you how it was:

"I sunk into a chair in the kitchen. I ate a dozen oatmeal cookies and chased them with a full pint of 1%. During this interlude, a small snowstorm blew in from the north. I peered out our bay window, watching these white wonders aimlessly drift. After what seemed an hour, I caught some movement by the garage near a snow drift. At first, I dismissed the entire incident. 'Probably the effects of the 2nd pint of 1%', I thought.

However, after another minute, I saw my first 12" *Frosted White* Snow trout. This is a rather rare Snow trout. (I know it was a Frosted White, because of the ever present frost on its lower jaw. It looks just like you do when you get off the trail after a five mile ski in zero-degree weather.)

"The old boy was going after a number 5 snowflake. Soon, he was joined by a snaggle of Frosted White Snow trout. Every last one of them was 12 to 14 inches. (If they wouldn't have had fins I'd have sworn they were gnomes.)

"I leaped out of my chair spilling the 1% on my wife's favorite rug. I grabbed my pole and sprinted out the front door. Unfortunately, in my excited state I forgot about the ice patch on the front step, which was now covered by snow. I lost my balance and unconsciously steadied myself with the 9 foot, 6 wt Orvis Hardbreaker. Well, that rod has now been renamed, 'Heartbreaker.' The tip and main shaft were splintered like kindling. I'm okay.

"Nevertheless, I did capture several snowflakes. I studied them. I went down into the workshop. After 3 hours, ten #5 hooks, 1 ounce of wool of an albino paca, I have produced, *'The White Wonder.'*

"Stay Tuned."

The next day Chris wrote, "White Wonder is a wipe out! Trout seem to be feeding on something in my tracks. Confused at best."

Well, it was obvious Chris didn't know quite as much about this species as Putz thought he did. P filled him in on what he suspected:

"Chris, a couple of things: First, congratulations on your astute identification of the Frosted White. They are indeed rare, and spotting the frost on the lower jaw is not an easy thing to do, particularly in a snowstorm.

"Next, it is not surprising that you did not have a lot of action on the trout with the White Wonder. Two reasons. First, snowflake flies are really impractical. We all know that no two flakes are alike, therefore you only have one drift to the trout, because if you float the same fly past that same trout again, it will know the flake is a fake because it has seen that pattern before. This immediately puts them off their feed.

"Second, I don't know if you know it, but the trout's main diet is snow fleas, otherwise identified as springtails. Now, springtails show up after a heavy snow has been around for a while. I think you waited too long to try the White Wonder. That might work during the heat of the storm, if you have a large enough snaggle to fish to, so you are not changing flies after every cast, but not later. Don't know. Never tried that.

"Back to the springtails. You can expect a hatch in late February and early March if we have a good year for snow, which of course we have not had this year. Why they have shown up this early? I can only speculate that they think we will be having an early spring and must reproduce now. The trout must know something too, so have begun to lay in some extra fat for the long migration north.

"Nonetheless, with this in mind, you must also realize that Snow trout are quite migratory, following the fleas and the snowfall. Therefore to harvest a Snow trout one must follow the snow line.

"Also, when fly fishing for Snow trout, your best bet is to sight fish. This means looking for the fleas when they hatch. It is impossible to see them in nymph stage as they are under the snow, but when they are hatching they are on the surface. They favor footprints and cross country ski trails. Although I have seen them in the web prints of snowshoes, but their numbers were not so great. Web prints act as a maze and confuse the poor little critters.

"The fly pattern required for this hatch is simple to tie. A #32 long shank Aberdeen seems to work best, but are almost impossible to find. I still have a few left from the old Herter's catalog days, but my supply is really dwindling and I keep them for emergency use only. The recipe goes like this: A #32 Aberdeen hook; black, extra, extra fine pure silk thread for the body, then one turn from the dark, under-the-neck hackle of the male rufus hummingbird. That's it!

"I must admit, I am teaching my granddaughter to tie flies specifically so she can tie this particular pattern for me as I am getting a bit old for this size.

"That's about it. Thanks for sharing your experience with me. I hope this will help your quest in the future. Keep in touch. Let's hit Columbia before the sap runs."

A few days later Putz received the following: "Hey, P, what do you know about snow peas? I have been researching and have heard it rumored that Snow trout will take snow peas if they are presented correctly. Any thoughts? Chris."

Putzer gave Chris an E for effort and P for persistence. He e-mailed him back: "You know if you are using two or more snow peas for bait, you might want to tie up some #12 caddis or one of my green sucker egg flies. Of course, suckers don't spawn for a bit, but the Snow trout might not know that. I would think that if you use live bait, the real peas might prove difficult to keep on the hook unless you encase a single pea on a # 14 hook and put them in the freezer overnight."

Three weeks and four snowfalls pass before Putz hears from his friend again. P had actually forgotten about his pursuit. His lament went like this: "Snow peas were a failure. The only thing raised were the eyebrows of curious and concerned neighbors."

"What about the snow fleas? You haven't told me if you tried the snow flea replicas yet," Putz zapped back.

"Couldn't find a #32 hook. Too late now. If you haven't noticed, it's 50 degrees outside. The sap is running. We'll get 'em next year."

Putz hadn't noticed; the sap was indeed running, but hey! He had a few #32's left, and he knew they were going to have at least one more storm before spring came for real. He figured he would tie up a few springtails that night—just in case he ran into some of those rare Frosted White Snow trout. You never know.

Until we meet in, on, or near the river,

Keep a good thought!

The Peshtigo Putzer

Columbia Lake

Even though Putz enjoys winter, he still gets the urge to fly fish. Here is one of the few places in Wisconsin where he scratches his itch.

Boy! I can't wait to get out on the water with the fly rod for bluegills and bass. I've got a fresh batch of flies tied and I'm ready! Too bad we're not rich; we could take off for a week and head south."

Thus stated a long-time friend of the P's, Chris, (of Snow trout fame) as he and Putzer shared breakfast and conversation one morning in late January.

"You want to go fly fishing? How comfortable are you in a canoe? Want to waste a day on a lake I just heard about last week?" P tosses out the questions as he sips from a steaming cup of English breakfast tea.

"Yes. Yes. And yes! And how far south do we have to drive?" Chris replies in chronological order.

"According to my information," Putz continues, "our destination will be just south of Portage, which is really northwest of here, not south. It is open water, fishable year round. It's called Columbia Lake, but it is really a cooling pond for the power plant. I am told we will be fishing in 70-plus degree water. I hear a lot of guys use float tubes because the water is so warm. The only problem I heard of is the fog, which is created when the warm water collides with the cold air. Want to give it a try?"

"You bet! When?"

"Well, how about Saturday?"

"Not good. How about two weeks from Friday?"

"I think that will work. Let me check my book." Putz reaches into his breast pocket and pulls out the ever-present date book. "Yep! That sounds like a plan."

And so it was on Friday, February the 13th, that two ice-bound, frustrated fly fishermen ventured forth from Grafton, Wisconsin on an overcast day with a light, damp, west wind. People did double takes as they headed out of town with a canoe on top of the old pickup truck.

The two hour drive was pleasant. There was snow on the ground all the way. They saw a few critters—a deer, couple of turkeys, squirrels—nothing special, but always nice to see. They wondered just what they would find at the lake.

"Well, all I know is Pat Ehlers fishes it for the hybrid strippers. The only place in Wisconsin where that kind of fishing is possible. He says it's worth the trip. That's good enough for me," stated P.

When they got to the lake, the fog, as promised, was rising from the water heavily. Visibility came and went. Sometimes it would be forty feet, sometimes a hundred, maybe a bit more.

They were dressed for winter as they launched the 16-foot Old Town, for it was 33 degrees with the promise of getting colder.

"Let's check out the water temp," said Chris, as Putzer began paddling.

A few feet from shore P flipped out a Squirrel Tail streamer to troll behind the canoe as he maneuvered along the dike.

"I don't believe this, the water is 84 degrees! What kind of fish are we going to catch here...Piranha?" the question came from Putzer's bow.

"I understand that has already been done a few years back. However, the sign in the parking lot said largemouth, smallmouth, and hybrid striped bass; along with bluegills, and catfish," P replied. "Get your line in the water. You can't catch fish with a thermometer."

Chris tied on a dark brown, #8 beadhead nymph of his own creation and cast toward the shore. Most of the time they fished a cast away from the shore's edge and could see beyond the shore a good distance. However, if they turned in their seats 90 degrees, they could only see to the end of their casts, sometimes not even that far.

The only visible structures were the rocks used to create the dike to form the lake. As they paddled along, they noticed action in the rocks—splashing and frolicking silver-sided fish, with a purplish iridescent appearance reflecting from their sides.

Putz and Chris presumed they were spawning, but what kind of fish they were, they had no idea. Perhaps these were the hybrids. Whatever they were, they were not interested in taking a fly. (Later they found out the fish were not the hybrid stripers, but probably shad.)

It only took about fifty yards of casting before Chris had his first fish—an eight-inch catfish caught on the nymph. An hour and several flies later he caught his second catfish, about the same size, this time on a cricket.

Putz had switched to an all-white Wiggle Bug, which he cast toward the rocks and slowly retrieved, allowing the bug to tantalize its way out from shore.

On about the sixth cast, "POW! POP! WHAM!" just like in the old Batman comics, a largemouth came completely out of the water to smash the white, struggling intruder.

After a lively battle, it was netted, measured, (14 inches) admired, and released.

They were now in sight of the power plant, at least occasionally, as often as the fog would allow. Chris checked the water temperature again—90 degrees.

P was now fishing a brown and white popper. He rolled it in toward the rocks, and was promptly rewarded with a smallmouth of similar size to his earlier cousin.

They had come to the end of this side of the lake where the fish refuge began. (Signs in the water told them that.)

They started to head for what they had been told was a "peninsula" running down the center of the lake, but the fog was so thick, that at one point they could not see any land mass whatsoever. Being first-timers, they choose caution instead of adventure, and turned around to retrace their steps.

Chris caught two bluegills on two different poppers on the return trip. For some reason neither fly fisher could catch more than one fish on any one pattern of fly. They couldn't explain that, although impatience may have had something to do with it. And they never did interest any of the frolicking spawners.

After three hours, in spite of the warm air rising around them, they both suddenly got chilled through and through from the dampness. They actually began to shiver. The air temperature was now in the mid 20's.

It was time to leave. Which they did.

On the drive back they warmed quickly with the truck heater going full blast for the first 40 miles. They concluded that it was a reasonably good day. Over a period of three hours they had caught two catfish, three bluegills, a largemouth and a smallmouth bass. Each fish was caught on a different fly. The bass were caught on the surface. There were no stripers, but...

"Hey!" they concluded, "not bad for a Friday the 13th in February."

Until we meet in, on, or near the river,

Keep a good thought!

The Peshtigo Putzer

Maple Sugaring

Spring! As much as P embraces winter, he looks forward to spring too. Heck, he looks forward to the change of all seasons, even summer, which is not his favorite. Of course, what he calls spring is not always what others think of as a sure sign of the "event." But then…P does operate a little differently than most, doesn't he? Join him and one of his granddaughters as they experience one of the first signs of spring.

What is your first sign of spring?" Putzer asks one of his granddaughters one afternoon as they are driving the back roads of Ozaukee County.

"What do you mean?" replies the young passenger.

"Well…I mean like…what signs in nature, when you see them, tell you that spring is coming?

"You know. Like, is it when we see skunk cabbage? Those wetland plants that thaw the soil around themselves with their own little internal furnaces, so they can push their pointed, purple-spotted heads through the ground to present the first flowers of the season to the world?

"Or, if you miss seeing the skunk cabbage, might it be when you see your first male red-winged blackbird and hear his cry, *'karee,'* as he sits and sways on last year's cattail, staking out a claim of territory for himself and a female, who will arrive at a later date?

"Or how about the first dark ribbons of open water showing in a snow-covered, ice-bound river? A river you know has fish staging at its mouth, getting ready for the run upstream to propagate their kind; and when they do you will be there trying to intercept a few with your fly rod? Or do you prefer to wait to fish until the ice on your favorite lake goes out?

"Are these your first signs of spring?"

The young rider's mouth begins to open, but not a word comes out before Putzer continues his litany.

"How about when you hear the sound of the male ruffed grouse drumming from his log, letting other males know this is his space and he will defend it, while at the same time telling the ladies he is ready to breed whenever they are.

"Meanwhile, big ol' Tom turkeys are gobbling and strutting the same song.

"Any and all of these happenings mean that spring is on the way, and that Ol' Man Winter is losing his grip."

Putz finally takes a breath, but not a big enough one to let his companion add anything to the one-sided conversation.

"Yes, young lady, these are all signs that spring is coming, but you know what the first sign is for me? Of course you do, because we are headed there right now aren't we? Of course we are.

The first sign of spring is when we can go out and tap the maples for their sap—Sugarin' Time! That's when spring begins for me."

Now he takes a really big deep breath and glances over at his charge for the day. She bobs her head up and down and quietly says, "Yes, Grampa," and that is all, for she knows this is going to be her grandfather's day.

She has been down this road before. She likes it, and she knows the best way to enjoy this day is not to interrupt and say very much. Perhaps a question or two if Grampa P forgets an important part of the story/activity of the day, which is unlikely, but possible. But until that time arrives, she will go along, smile, add a "That's good" or "Why?" or "I like that," every now and again, but that is all that she is required to do.

They will both have a good day in the woods and Grampa P will glow inwardly as they pass through the entire process of making sap into syrup. It won't take long, an hour or so, because the trees have been tapped for weeks and enough sap has been collected so the cooking process has been started at the nature center they are about to visit.

They pull into the parking lot and get out of the truck. The Sugar Inn is just over the hill, down the path.

Rising through the leafless tree tops, they can see steam from the evaporator (cooker). They walk the trail to the wood building, which is both the beginning and the end of the self-guided, hands-on tour.

A staff person gives them a hand brace and bit, a small bleach bottle, two spiels (the little metal spouts that the bucket or bag hangs from, and the sap flows through), a hammer, a bucket and a bag, and then directs them down the path to the trees that still require tapping.

"Looks like a perfect day," Putz says. "When the sun is high, and temperatures are in the 40's, after a night below freezing, like it was last night, and the wind is low, that's when the sap flows. We should be able to tap a tree and see the sap run right down the spile into the bucket today. If it happens, we can taste the sap directly from the tree."

"That's good," adds granddaughter, smiling.

They find a proper size tree, one they can hug, and take the brace and bit and start drilling on a little upward angle. After drilling about two inches they stop, remove the bit, dragging the chewed wood fibers out of the hole by moving the bit head in and out a few times.

Then, before inserting the spile, they spray a little bleach into the hole to prevent bacteria from hurting the tree. That done, they "tap" in the spile lightly with the hammer, and hang the bucket on its lip.

"Now let's wait a few minutes to see if the sap will begin to flow right away," instructs Putz.

It doesn't even take a minute before they hear the ping...ping...pang—drip, drip, dripping of sap into the bucket.

"I told you it would be a good day for this!" states P, with that grin of confidence. "Now remove the bucket and put your mouth under the spile and let some sap drip into your mouth."

Granddaughter does as she is told, and soon she has clear sap dripping onto her lips and tongue. It is not very sweet. After a few "catches" they replace the bucket and look for another tree.

"Grampa," she asks. "Why doesn't the sap taste very sweet?"

"Well, that is why it has to be cooked," answered Putz. "You see, on an average, it takes 40 gallons of sap to make one gallon of syrup. That's why you don't put it on pancakes directly from the tree. Let's tap another one."

They find another hugger and do it all over again, but this time hang the bag instead of the bucket.

"This shows people that there is more than one kind of container you can use to collect the sap. Actually, bags keep the sap cleaner," says Putz. "The downside is that squirrels can chew holes in bags—they can't in buckets."

They follow the trail back through the sugarbush. (A sugarbush is what a woods full of hard maples tapped for the sap is called.) As they walk, Putzer explains that all across Wisconsin, beginning in February in the south, where they are, and running into late April in the far north, people are taking to the maple woods for this annual spring ritual.

"Just think," Putz said. "If we lived in Wishigan Country, we could tap our own trees and make our own syrup on our own land. Of course, it would be more work, but sometime I would like to try it, I think."

Back at the Sugar Inn, one of the naturalists is explaining the entire process.

"Once the sap gets running, and the collector tanks are full, the cooking begins," he says. "Cookers vary in size and design. Commercial companies use gas. Nature centers, like ours, cook with wood. I know some individuals who use electric fry pans to reduce the sap to syrup right in their kitchens.

"Whichever cooking process is used, the idea is to make a light brown colored, quality syrup," he continues.

"Today, we test the sap with either a candy thermometer or a syrup hydrometer.

"When the temperature is seven degrees above the boiling point of water, approximately 219 degrees, or the specific gravity of the boiling liquid floats the bulb properly in the hydrometer, we have syrup.

"Notice, when speaking of boiling, I said 'approximately,' because water boils at different temperatures depending on conditions of the day."

Then he gives a little history lesson.

"In days past, prior to thermometers and hydrometers, the apron method was used by pioneers and Indians. The people doing the cooking would dip a spoon into the pot and watch the liquid as it ran off the spoon. If it flowed looking like an apron, instead of in drips, it was ready to be drawn off for bottling."

Then he demonstrated.

"Whatever the method, past or present, everybody likes the smell of evaporating sap, just as we have right here." He waves his hand through the rising steam.

Putzer leans over and whispers to his granddaughter, "Can you smell the sap? The air is so heavy today, I not only smell it, I can taste it in the steam."

Off to the side of the building another wood fire is burning. This one is under a grill with a very large flat metal top. At the grill, a man with a name tag that identifies him as *"Father Fire"* is cooking small sausages and pancakes.

On a side table are: paper plates, plastic forks, paper napkins, paper cups, a jar of instant coffee, instant hot chocolate, tea bags, a large metal pitcher full of fresh-made syrup, and a dish of dill pickles.

"Now," announces the naturalist, "You are all invited to try a sausage and pancake, have a cup of coffee, tea, or hot chocolate made with hot sap drawn from the evaporator, and a dill pickle. Be sure to dip the dill pickle in the syrup before taking a bite, and don't worry because the pancakes are green. That is in honor of St. Patrick's birthday, March 17th."

"Grampa," granddaughter starts to say, "isn't St. Patrick's Day your…" but she is cut off.

"Never mind, child. Grampa Putzer doesn't have birthdays anymore. Forget that last thought, and don't finish the sentence," he says rather sternly.

"OK, but I think it's neat to have all these people honoring someone on your birthday with green pancakes and dill pickles. It just kinda fits somehow." She pauses, smiles, and continues, "I'll be quiet now, and eat my lunch."

On the way back to the truck Putzer wraps his arm around her shoulder. She looks up and says, "I didn't spoil your day did I? With the mention of your…you know…B-day?"

"Nah, you could never spoil my day."

Until we meet in, on, or near the river,

Keep a good thought!

The Peshtigo Putzer

Dancing Chickens

Normally, the Putzers visit one of their favorite wildlife watching sites, Crex Meadows Wildlife Area, at Grantsburg, Wisconsin, in the fall. This year, 2000, they, actually Putz, decided he wanted to go in spring so he could watch the Prairie Chickens dance their mating dance. Naturally, Mrs. P went along.

"You know," P says to his better half, "we won't be able to camp in April. They (meaning Crex Meadows Wildlife Area) only allow camping from September through December."

"You mean...we won't be able to crawl in and out of the back of the truck on our hands and knees everytime we need or want something?" Mrs. P replied with a definite note of sarcasm. "What a shame! I will certainly miss that."

"That, I take, means a motel with a bed and shower is alright with you then?" was P's reply, with a knowing smile on his face.

He made the reservations.

Perhaps this would be a good time to explain how one goes about watching prairie chickens dance: One watches from a blind. A blind that must be reserved in advance. The blind is generally made from canvas or similar material. It is approximately four feet high, four feet wide, and six to eight feet long. It has a roof and a 2 x 12 plank, raised ten inches off the ground, to sit on. There are "peep holes" or "lens ports" for observing and/or photographing the birds. Observers are assigned a specific blind, by number, and must be in said blind before sunrise. (The ranger designates the time.) Observers stay in the blind until the birds are completely done with their dancing and fooling around, and leave the "booming grounds."

After checking into their motel, the Ps drove to the ranger station. It was about 4:30 in the afternoon. Their "blind date" was tomorrow. They hoped to talk to someone about the wheres and whats of the day. No one was around. The sign on the door said the crew was out doing a controlled burn—a tool used to manage the grasslands in the area.

"Guess we will just have to find out as we go," Putz said. "We better have a look at where our blind is."

Putz followed the map, which had been included with their reservation and instructions.

They found their blind at the edge of a field about 100 yards from the road. They each made note of the landmarks so they could find the same spot in the dark the next morning.

From there, they drove to their favorite overlook, at Reisinger Lake. (This is where they camp in fall.) Along the way, deer were everywhere. The swans, geese, ducks, and sandhill cranes they were accustomed to seeing were there too, albeit in lesser numbers than in fall. The northern migration was in full swing.

A marsh hawk hunted, skimming the grass and cattail tops, keeping an eye out for supper. It was good to be visiting again the Ps agreed. They spent over an hour, just watching everything and "everyone."

The alarm went off at 3:45 A.M. The drive to the blind went fine. (Oh, there was a tad of grumbling, something about "...better be worth all this," but nothing out of the ordinary.)

They found the blind with the aid of flashlights, and crawled inside. It was a cozy fit.

"Do you really need all this camera gear? I have hardly any room on this bench," mentioned Mrs. P, as Putz was arranging his gear in the dark.

"Ouch! You just about poked my eye out with that thing!"

"Sorry. Now please keep your voice in a whisper. According to the information sheet the birds should be coming any time now."

The Ps were finally settled in the blind, with tripod and cameras, by 5:16.

The birds announced their arrival with the "vroom, vroom, vroom" at 5:18. This was followed by a shadow streaking across the horizon, such as it was at that time of the morning. Then another shadow was "seen."

"Vroom, Vroom, Brrrrrrr, (the rapid staccato stomping of little prairie chicken feet) chip...chirp...cheep, vroom." Sounds from around the blind.

The sun officially rose at 6:04. Putz started taking photos at 5:58 with a reddening sky for a background. He shot the last of his "Sunrise/Prairie Chicken" images as the sun peeked through the trees.

As the sun rose, the Ps could finally really see the birds distinctly. All told, seven, maybe eight, different males, and one to three females came to be observed. It was difficult to make an accurate count because the little "chickens" kept coming and going, especially the females. Never were all of the birds on the field at the same time.

The males would strut and puff and stomp and boom, and protect a specific territory they had "staked out"—an area perhaps eight feet square. When another male came near the "property line," the "owner" would rush over to defend.

The females just kind of wandered around aimlessly, checking the boys out, but on this particular morning no lady gave the slightest hint that she was ready to mate. They really looked quite bored, or so it seemed to the Ps. They saw no copulations. (They were required to report the numbers of birds, by sex, and the number of copulations seen as part of the bargain for renting the blind.)

The birds left the grounds around 7:50. The Ps left the blind at 8:05. They walked a bit stiff and hunched over for the first few yards on the way back to the truck.

The temperature, when they crawled out of bed, had been 37 degrees. They had dressed appropriately, and only their feet froze. The rest of their bodies, because they could not move much and were sitting rather low to the ground and bent over in the short-walled, low-ceilinged blind, just got numb.

Back at the motel, the hot shower felt mighty good, and they each tarried under it for a goodly length of time.

"Well, what do you think of the experience?" Putz inquired of his spouse over a hearty breakfast.

"Like most ideas you come up with, it was out of the ordinary, but I'm glad I did it," replied Mrs. P, feeling much better now that she was warm and getting some nourishment.

"So, should we see if we can go again tomorrow?"

"You go right ahead. Wake me when you get back."

Until we meet in, on, or near the river,

Keep a good thought!

The Peshtigo Putzer

Birding from Canoes

The Ps are always trying to add to their Birding Life List. On this outing they canoe the Sheboygan Marsh, hoping to add a species or two.

"What a gorgeous morning," stated Mrs. P as they drove up to the edge of the launch site. "What beautiful fog. It is going to be outstanding, once the sun gets up a little higher."

"For sure," was all P could add without duplicating her already expressive description of what was in front of them. "Let's unload. I'm sure Scott will be here with the others soon."

They slid out of the truck and began unloading the canoe from the top of the pickup, then reloading it with their birding gear—binoculars, field books, and cameras. Once all was in order, they sat on the tailgate, facing the marsh, opened a couple of granola bars, sipped coffee and tea, and waited.

The Ps are at the Sheboygan Marsh in Southeast Wisconsin. They are participating as volunteers for the Outdoor Skills and Education Center (OSEC), of Plymouth, Wisconsin (since moved to Sheboygan Falls) for a morning of bird watching from canoes—not an exceptional outing, but not a common one either.

If you are unfamiliar with Southeast Wisconsin, the Sheboygan Marsh is about two miles west, as the crow flies, of Elkhart Lake, a small town nationally known for its auto race track, Road America.

The marsh is a portion of the Ice Age National Scientific Reserve, and is considered an archaeological treasure, lying at the northern extreme of the Kettle Moraine area, and it has a valuable, rich, deep Native American history.

Because of these geological and historical features, the marsh and surrounding landscape are currently being used as a natural outdoor classroom, as well as for hunting, fishing, and other assorted recreational uses.

OSEC is one organization using this as a classroom, and the Putzers were a part of one of those classes on this particular morning.

The P's job was to assist any of the other birders who were not familiar with canoes to become comfortable sitting and paddling said craft. In other words, give a brief "class."

They would also help with bird identification, if necessary, and would paddle "sweep," meaning last canoe, so no one would get lost—not very likely this morning.

As it turned out, the Putzers were one-fourth of the entire birding group, with Scott Johnson, the Director of OSEC, and his assistant, John Rank being another fourth. What that means is that only four other people were willing to get up before dawn, drive to the marsh, and enjoy a sunrise, from the water, the third week of May. This would be the easiest volunteer job they ever participated in.

"It's a dirty job, but someone has to do it," Putz said to Scott as they were discussing the plan for the day.

As the rest of the party arrived, the Ps readied the other canoes. When everyone was comfortable and set, four canoes pushed off from the landing, easing gently into the fog.

As the fog engulfed them, and the sun became dim-to-lost at their backs, they paddled down the main channel toward the lake.

"Look out for the islands if the wind comes up! Don't let one sneak up on you," Scott tells everyone as he passes them taking the lead. Everyone nods, then gives him a funny look.

"Watch out for the islands?" Mrs. P questions.

"Yeah," P answers. "They float, and move with the current toward the dam. A strong wind can blow them all over the place. Some of them are small enough so they can actually move fast enough to bump into someone who is not paying attention. No need to worry unless it gets really windy. Even then, they are not going to race down on you and tip the canoe. It's just another neat thing about this marsh...or on a morning like this, should I refer to it as a fen?"

The bird sightings went along pretty normally—Canada geese, ring-billed gulls, several species of ducks, red-winged blackbirds—the usual fare.

There had been some talk about seeing yellow-headed blackbirds here. This would be exciting for the Ps, because P has only seen one, a few years ago, and Mrs. P has never seen any.

The group had been out about a half hour, when word came down the line that there were indeed yellow-heads in the area.

It wasn't long and Putz heard the croaking "song" of the said bird—a raspy, hoarse "Kroak."

A little reconnaissance and they saw their "prey"—a very colorful male sitting on a cattail some twenty yards ahead.

Naturally, Putz wanted to photograph it.

With Mrs. P in the bow, they eased forward. They would float quietly, moving forward with only an occasional dip of the paddle. Between strokes, P would place his paddle carefully, silently across the thwart and snap images.

P was wearing a camo jacket. Mrs. P's jacket was bright yellow! They were able to get within ten feet of the bird before it took off.

"Boy," said P, "he really let us get close. I wonder if that poor yellow-head was confused. Maybe, because of the color of your jacket, he thought he was seeing a really big, bright, beautiful female approaching. I'll bet he thought he could persuade you into nesting with him this spring. Why else would he let us get so close?

"Of course," Putz continued to ramble and hypothesize, "as we got closer, he realized that the yellow color was completely covering your entire front, head, and back, instead of just the breast. This would not be good, in his mind. This would only mean that a new male was planning on taking over his territory.

"Well, far be it from him to do battle with some fella who was a thousand times his size, so he moved on. What do you think?"

"I think you think too much!" declared Mrs. P. "Keep paddling; we are falling behind. We are supposed to keep track of everyone, remember?"

As the morning progressed, the fog lifted. They saw their first-ever marsh wren, a brilliantly-colored orange and black American redstart, and a couple of soras. (Sora is a member of the rail family, but, for some reason, "rail" is not included in its name, as it is when referring to a Virginia rail, for example.)

One sora was tucked away up a narrow cut no wider than the length of the Old Town—16 feet. The path was a dead end, and it required backing out instead of turning around.

Back at the landing, "the staff," meaning the Putzers, Scott and John, bid goodbye to the other four members of the group who rose early, then headed for the restaurant and a well-deserved late breakfast.

While waiting for their meal, it was determined that it was an excellent outing. Everyone had a good time.

P felt especially fortunate that the male yellow-head did not decide to try to seduce his wife into its nest. He might have been successful.

"She could have left me right then and there," he theorized. "Then, my Lord, I hate to think of it, but I would have had to paddle the canoe back to the landing by myself."

Until we meet in, on, or near the river,
Keep a good thought!

The Peshtigo Putzer

The Other Door County

By now you know the Putzers enjoy the outdoors in many more ways than hunting and fishing. Here is another example of how viewing the countryside from the saddle of a bike can be just as enjoyable as from the seat in a canoe.

What are you doing?" Putzer asked the financial director, household planner, and occasional tour guide of their family—the irrepressible Mrs. P.

"I'm surfing for a B&B. If we are going to Door County for a couple days of biking, I want to go in style for a change. If I'm going to straddle a small, sadistically-designed seat all day, I want clean sheets spread over a sensually soft mattress to lay my strained sinew and blemished bones on when nighttime rolls around. I'm tired of camping every time we go somewhere. I am getting tired of sleeping in the back of the truck on an air mattress that ends up flat around midnight. Any objections?"

"No. Not as long as it comes out of your spending money," P replied simply. "You find what you want. You make the arrangements. Then just point me in the right direction when the time comes to leave the driveway. Might you be planning on spending all four nights in excessive luxury?"

"No, I think just two. We can travel *"Your Way"* the other two nights," she said with a smile. "I just want to do this trip a little bit differently."

"OK! How about if we stay at Potawatomi State Park the first night, B&B the next two, and the Wagon Trail on Friday?"

"That's good."

And so it was that the P's annual bike hike would be at least somewhat different than those of past years.

They left home about 9:45 a.m. and arrived at Potawatomi some two and a half hours later. After touring the park six times to determine a proper campsite, they registered and set up camp, after which they headed out to explore the immediate area.

They looked for, and found, the Sherwood Point Lighthouse, a subject portrayed on many of the area promotional brochures. This is a Coast Guard-operated lighthouse, and the family that operates it lives on the grounds.

A sign requiring all visitors to "STOP" and turn around and respect the privacy of the family, removed the possibility of Putz being able to capture an image or two. (The promotional photos were taken from the water and the Ps had not brought their boat. Next time. Maybe. If they remember.)

They toured a few back roads, then reentered the park, checking out its perimeter as they returned, slowly, to camp.

They found wonderful picnic areas along the shore of Sturgeon Bay, where sailing ships and yachts and small fishing boats pass throughout the day, and an observation tower that overlooks Sawyer Harbor.

There was a small airport near the park, and as they pulled into their campsite, between five and six p.m., the skies overhead were buzzing with small planes.

"They must fly to and from work," said Mrs. P, reflecting on the many elegant homes they had seen in the area.

After supper, a campfire chased the chill from the early autumn air, and provided reading light for both.

In the morning P wiggled out of his sleeping bag. Fall was definitely in the air. A sweatshirt was welcome.

A full day was planned. They would be biking the first leg of the Ahnapee Trail, 18 miles one way, and, of course, they needed to go both directions, because they had no shuttle service.

The bike book said the trailhead was at Sawyer Park. That may be true, but the Ps could not find it. They followed a sign along highways 42/57 that directed them to the trail. They found the trail, but no place to park.

While wandering back and forth looking for the parking lot, a gentleman from the area stopped and asked if they were lost. (They must have looked as confused as they were.) They explained, and he said, "Follow me," and led them to the trail lot—a spot they had passed several times. (On their behalf, there were no signs indicating it was a trail parking lot.)

It was cloudy when the Ps hit the path. The wind picked up a bit and was quartering into their faces.

"If it stays from this direction, we will have it on our backs on the return trip," Putz calculated. (Want to bet it switched?)

After an hour, the blue sky showed and the sweatshirts came off. It was a great day!

(The trail traverses two counties, Door and Kewaunee, covering 28 miles, one way, from Sturgeon Bay to Casco. It is an old railroad bed made of crushed gravel. Peddling is not difficult except for a mile and a half where the trail is shared with horses. Horses and bikes do not mix.)

The Ps passed through a variety of country that day—farms, prairie, wetlands, woods, and orchards. At times they paralleled the Ahnapee River.

The only downer of the day was the aforementioned section that was shared by horses. Not only was the trail bed chewed up by the hooves, one also had to try to avoid the "horse apples."

This did not always happen, and at one point Putz was getting bogged down in the soft, "hoof-tilled" trail when his front wheel twisted and he went down. Fortunately...well, not really...he had a "soft" landing.

Mrs. P walked her bike the last quarter mile.

On a brighter note, their day was full of blue sky dotted with cumulus clouds. The wildflowers—deep yellow goldenrod, white asters and Queen Ann's lace, orange-spotted jewelweed, purple thistles and swamp milkweed, blue and white variegated gentians, fuzzy old-man's-beard, and even a late blooming orange hawkweed—waved and smiled as the Ps passed.

In the fields were squash and pumpkin. The orchards held rosy red, juicy apples. There were hawks and hayfields, and a mama great blue heron was still teaching her youngster how to survive. It must have hatched late, because the fledgling was still looking pretty scraggly, although it could fly a little.

There was a snowmobile memorial shelter, which offered protection from the weather if required, and deer stands were all over the place.

Every now and then along the side of the trail, little signs told the history of the original railway, the Ahnapee & Western.

They had left the parking lot at 9:45 in the morning and returned at 3:45. The odometer on Mrs. P's Trek 720 registered 33.5 miles. They felt it. They were hot. Sweaty.

They loaded the bikes on the back of the truck and headed for the night's place of residence—the Hearthside Farm Bed & Breakfast—and a shower.

Hearthside Farm was just that, a semi-retired farm, run by Lu and Don Klussendorf, semi-retired farmers with very interesting stories to tell.

Their room was magnificent, with a poster bed so tall Putz didn't have a clue as to how they got it into the room.

"Maybe they built the room around the bed," he commented.

The shower was two steps lower than the rest of the bathroom, with a slate floor and walls of stone. Just a bit different than camping.

After unloading and a shower the Ps asked their hosts about good places to eat. Lu suggested several, in a variety of price ranges.

The Ps opted for a gourmet restaurant in the Sturgeon Bay historic district. They were not disappointed. Mrs. P had: beef tenderloin with portabella mushrooms and a spicy smoked red chili rum sauce, and goat cheese mashed potatoes. While Putz opted for: wild boar chops complimented with crispy gorgonzola polenta, wild mushroom shallot ragout, and sun dried tomato jam. Both entrees were terrific. The cherry pie, however, left something to be desired. (But then, no one makes pie crust like the Putzers.)

It was late, eight o'clock, when they returned to "the Farm." It had been a long day. The living room was inviting, but the bed was more so. They slept well, on clean sheets spread over a sensually soft mattress.

An important part of B&B-ing is the second B—breakfast.

The host, Don, proved his worth as a cook. He required two hours to prepare breakfast, which always included fresh fruit, homemade jams, bread, coffee cake, and muffins. (One morning they had pancakes made with buckwheat and sorghum, and bacon; the second morning, it was eggs and crisp fried potatoes.)

The second day on the trail began cloudy with showers

predicted on and off. It was also windy. Fortunately, only 9.6 miles one way was the required peddle.

They did get wet, but not too wet. While waiting out one shower under a group of trees, P glanced down and there, on his raincoat, sat a red and black dragon fly, a calico pennant. It had found the only dry spot around, thanks to the brim of Putz's hat and the hood on his raincoat and the angle of the rain.

The calico just sat there, perfectly content, working its little front "feet" over and around its head, as if it were doing everything possible to keep that part of its body totally dry. (Or maybe it had an itch that needed scratching.)

Anyway, after five minutes the rain stopped and the Ps continued on their way—with nothing else earthshaking happening.

That night they walked the historic district, did a little shopping, saw the beginning stages of the building process on two huge yachts in a "building barn," and admired another massive "ship" moored along the dock, which looked like it was ready to sail.

"Probably going to one of the oil sheiks," P commented. (It was that big and luxurious-looking.)

During the stroll, Putz stepped off the curb into a hole. He limped for a few blocks, but fortunately it was nothing serious.

"I see you have not lost your nimbleness," commented Mrs. P after she saw that he would not require any special care.

"What can I say?"

They ate at a meat and potatoes restaurant where the bill for dinner, including tip, was under $20. Mrs. P treated.

They spent their second night in that same bed, had their second breakfast, then headed north to the "tip of the Door."

That night they slept in the truck, with the sounds of the night all around.

Back home, Mrs. P asked, "Well, did you miss camping all four nights?"

"Well, I must admit, B&B-ing has some good points. I don't

think we will give up traveling in the truck, but *My Way* will no longer be the only way we travel. Besides taking the B&B expenses out of your money was a nice change."

Until we meet in, on, or near the river,

Keep a good thought!

The Peshtigo Putzer

Turkeys or Trout? Why Not Both?

Here is a perfect example of how P tries very hard to squeeze as much out of an opportunity as he can. He deliberately puts himself into a situation where he must make difficult choices: Should he hunt or fish? As is his nature, he will try to do both. But, will either be successful?

Putzer had always wanted to fish one of the premier trout streams of southwest Wisconsin—the West Fork of the Kickapoo, but, because the Ps live in southeast Wisconsin, and have seasonal property in Wishigan Country, a trip to the West Fork, though not out of the question, does require an overnight stay or two.

To most, this would not be a problem, but...Putz is a frugal individual, so if he is going to invest in a couple days of out-of-the-pocket expenses, he tries to make such a trip one that combines two or more interests, and one that has the potential for repaying itself, over time, with some good photos and maybe a line or two for a sellable tale.

A few years back, such an opportunity presented itself.

If Putz could pull a Zone 3 Turkey Permit during the second or third season, he could put together a trip that would allow him to fish this category 5 trout stream while trying to pop a gobbler at the same time.

With that in mind, Putz applied accordingly.

(Perhaps this would be a good time to explain two things to non-Wisconsinites or those of you who do not fish or hunt.

First, we here in Wisconsin have an early trout season, on selected streams, which is catch and release, artificial, barbless hooks only; and our turkey hunting is by permit only, which must be applied for by season—six, five day sessions with Mondays and Tuesdays off between each season—and by zone, of which there are forty-some. The applications must be in by the 10th of December and the hunt starts in April.

Knowing this, you now understand that putting a trip like this together is not necessarily difficult, but does require some advanced thought.)

When P's turkey permit arrived, he found he had the zone he wanted, but not his first choice of seasons. Nor his second.

"Oh well, at least the fourth season might be a bit warmer than the others," he rationalized to himself. "This could be important, because I plan to tent." (Little did he know how right that statement would be.)

The morning of departure, the day before the opening of his turkey season, arrived. P packed the trout tackle, turkey trappings, camping comforts, and photo paraphernalia, and headed west to Wildcat Mountain State Park. Mrs. P decided not to go on this trip—other commitments, she said. (Actually, she would not have had enough to do. She didn't hunt turkeys, and fished trout only limitedly. Sitting in a tent for four, five days, mostly alone, was not her idea of fun!)

Putz arrived early in the afternoon. He set up camp, scouted the area for hunting possibilities, then made supper.

As the sun was setting, P was at the overlook scoping out the valley below. The Kickapoo River wound its way through the countryside. From his vantage point, he could see three toms and two hens feeding their way across a newly-plowed and planted field several miles away.

"An omen of success, or just a perfect end to the day?" P pondered. "Time will tell."

Earlier in the day, between camp set up and supper, Putz had found an attractive looking field to hunt. He was there bright and early Wednesday morning, along with a whip-poor-will and two gobblers. The toms were a long way off, and try as he may, Putz could not seduce either of them to show.

Putz was back to camp by 9:30. The temperature was already 72 degrees, heading for a high of 84.

P put on shorts and a light T-shirt and headed for the Kickapoo Valley Reserve office in La Farge to pick up his permit so he could roam the Reserve legally and freely.

(The Kickapoo Valley Reserve, some 8569 acres of land, was purchased from private landowners in the 1960's so a dam could be built to "resolve" the flooding problems of the area. The project was started, but economic problems and after-the-fact "discoveries" prevented it from being finished. Nature took a hand in reclaiming what the US Army Corps of Engineers had disrupted. Eventually, management of 7500 acres of the land was turned over to the State of

Wisconsin and 1200 acres to the Ho-Chunk Nation, the former Native American residents.)

After leaving the office and receiving some tips on where to fish, P headed west on Highway 82 until he crossed the West Fork of the Kickapoo at County Highway S.

P found the parking lot he was told was there for fishermen, and found a gentleman halfway into, or out of, his waders.

"Are you coming or going?" P asked.

"Leaving."

"How was the fishing?" P inquired further.

"Okay, I picked up a dozen or so. Nothing big—seven to nine inches—but pretty fish. Browns. The water is really warm for this time of the year. They seem to be quite active."

"Mind telling me what you were using?"

"Not at all. A beadhead Scud. Number 12. Olive. Here, do you have one like this? If not, I can let you have one of mine."

"Thanks, but I do have a couple that look like that. Were you fishing up or down from here?"

"Both. There are some nice pools below here. You going to try it here?"

"Not sure. I've never fished this stream before. Thought I'd drive up along the road and look over a few spots before I give it a try."

"Good idea. There is a lot of good water here. Good luck!" Then he slipped in behind the wheel of his car and was gone.

Putz took a brief look at the water the man had just fished, returned to his truck, and headed up Cty. S. He drove through Avalanche and continued until he found Bloomingdale Road. This path follows and crosses the West Fork several times. At each crossing P got out and looked. At every bridge he saw fish. Trout-type fish.

Along this section of river, from the parking lot where P met the fellow fisherman, north until Bloomingdale Road, the river was running clear with a good current. It was perhaps sixteen to twenty feet wide, and except for undercut banks and some deep holes here and there, it ran quite shallow. Beautiful riffles wound through farmland with ample access points.

Putz selected a stretch of stream mid-way between Avalanche and Bloomingdale. There was a wide shoulder pull-off, which he could tell others had used for the same purpose. A slightly used trail led to the river.

It was now 80-plus degrees. Chest-high waders were not an option. P pulled on a pair of old, thin, long pants over his shorts and slipped into his hip boots.

His rod was a six foot, eight inch, two weight St. Croix. P attached a seven and a half foot 6X leader and because the water was so clear, added three feet of 6X Mirage tippet, to which he tied a #12 olive, beadhead Scud.

"Might as well begin with what they want," he said to himself.

There was a good hundred to hundred and fifty feet of marshy grass and willows separating the road from the stream. Negotiation was not difficult if you remembered to lift your feet above the grass. P did not always remember, and the inevitable "trip up" almost sent him to the hospital with a stick in the eye. Fortunately, it only skinned his cheek.

Putz did not wade to begin with. He fished from the bank from a kneeling position, because there were fish directly in front of him and to wade would be to spook.

This section of stream had grass and weeds growing very near the edge of the bank, but casting was not too difficult if Putz kept his casts high.

Putz could see eight fish, facing the current. It looked like they were just enjoying the sun and warmth. They did not appear to be feeding. Putz cast the beadhead up and let it drift and bump slowly down to where two were finning close together.

It would be nice to say that one rushed over and smashed his offering, but that didn't happen. Actually, he fished that school for a half hour.

Finally, he switched to a #14 gold beadhead white scud, and on the fourth drift, a nine-inch brown hit the fly like it was really hungry. A fun battle ensued. P landed the fish, snapped a quick photo, and released it. It swam right back to where it was stationed before. Obviously, these fish had territories and said territories were honored by their peers.

It was so neat for Putz to see the entire event—the strike, the fight, and the release. Normally, he does not have sight fishing opportunities for small stream trout.

Putz ran the fly by the other fish for a while and then moved on. He never caught another fish on that fly.

"So," P questioned, "was it the fly pattern that triggered the strike or was the fish just hungry and took whatever came along? Maybe I irritated it enough by continuous drifting that it just got mad. Who knows?"

Fifty yards downstream P found three fish feeding in a riffle. He could watch them hold next to a small rock then dash out, grab something, and return to "their spot." It was so much fun watching them, he almost forgot to fish.

One fish on the opposite bank, right next to the grass, was rising to something. Putz couldn't see anything on the water. A friend of P's insists that these fish exist on midges. He fishes with #18's to #22's.

"Are they feeding on midges?" P asks himself.

P does not carry flies that small. Heck, he can't even see the eye of a #22, much less tie one on the end of a tippet. He did have a couple of #16's that this friend had given him, so after trying some small nymphs with no success, Putz tied on a #16 Adams and made his approach.

Putz positioned himself at the center of a shallow rock bar where he could lower his profile by kneeling while having the openness of the creek bed to back cast into.

Upstream, in front of P, the river cut sharply to his left creating an undercut bank from which the fish was feeding.

P waited for the fish to rise again, then dropped the little grey and brown fly about two feet above the rise. The fly alighted gently on the water and began its drift. Nothing. Another cast, another drift, another nothing. He waited. The trout rose again from the same location. Putz had not put him down.

The next cast P put right up against the grass, bouncing the fly off the strings of old brown blades before it alighted and made its short drift. This time the trout took. Not a hard smash, rather that classic little dimple that only a trout can make.

Putz took in the slack; the little hook set itself with the tension. It was a quick, wild fight once Putz got the trout out of the little hole and into the pebble riffle. Another brown about nine inches.

Below him now was a much bigger and deeper pool. He worked that water for all it was worth, because although he could not see anything feeding, he was certain there was a really good-sized fish in there.

After an hour and four fly changes, P gave up and fished his way back upstream to where he began.

The last fly he had tied on for that big pool was one of his own concoctions of some forty years ago. It represents no special distinct food source, but rather simulates most nymphs. He called it the Rapids Nymph. P fished a #12. He fished this pattern all the way back to the truck.

Below a narrow fast drop in the tail of a run, and from under an undercut bank, he hit the trout of the day. (More correctly, the trout did the hitting.) It measured a full twelve inches of native brook trout. P doesn't believe there is a more beautiful fish in the entire state of Wisconsin than a wild, native brookie.

He admired and photographed it carefully, then sent it back home. A good way to end the day. And end it then he did.

The sun was setting as P finished dishes from a well-earned supper cooked on the good ol' two-burner Coleman.

He did not fish on Thursday. He dedicated that day to turkey hunting.

Have you ever hunted in full camo, including mask, in 88 degree weather from five a.m. to five p.m., with no guarantee that the showers back at the campground would be working? Trust me, P loves hunting, but…

Suffice to say, the best part of the day was when he returned to camp, and found the showers were up and running.

He had heard only two gobblers. He did have a hen almost walk into his lap. It was five feet from his right toe. It never even looked at him. Was he camoed well or what?

Putz's original plan was to leave on Saturday, but when he found out that the campsites were all reserved for the weekend, he knew Friday night and Saturday morning would be a zoo. He hunted a few hours Friday morning, broke camp, and took off for home.

On the way, he stopped to fish the West Fork one more time. The trout were still where they were before, but they were not in the striking mood. He guessed that the sudden out-of-the-ordinary hot weather had gotten to them as it had to Putz.

When he got home, Mrs. P greeted him with, "Well, do we have meat for the table?"

"Well, not exactly." He related, in brief, the circumstances.

"So, did any good come from the trip? Looks like all I missed was sleeping on a deflated air mattress."

"Oh, I think you would have found a few things you would have enjoyed. Wait 'till you see the photos."

Until we meet in, on, or near the river,

Keep a good thought!

The Peshtigo Putzer

Of Hats and Images, It's Tough to Change

What do hats have to do with the outdoors? Outdoor people always need something to keep the sun and rain off their heads. And some, like Putz, like to have an image. His hat plays a big part of that image.

It was a few years back, as I remember.

He said he'd been thinking about it for about three months. After all, it was a major decision, not one to do on the spur of the moment. It was the kind of thought that had to sit for a while before it is ready to come forth, like a good beer going through the fermentation period.

First, he had to ask, did he really need a new one? After all, the old one had been serving him well for a good many years.

Actually, it had become an icon. People recognized him by it—sometimes from great distances. It would be difficult to replace.

But, on the other side of the coin, its age was becoming the problem, even for him. It's not that he was ashamed of it, but he had cleaned it to a point where even bleach would not make it bright and white any more, and the problem was that the dirt was not uniform, so that it really looked blotchy and ugly—kinda disgusting. (Mrs. P did mention, on occasion, that this was really a reflection of himself.)

Still, he waited. He just could not find what he thought he was looking for.

I caught him one day paging through catalogs. "What are we looking for today Putz?" I inquired as I pulled up a chair. "How do you plan on spending your wife's hard-earned money this time?" (Mrs. P was still working, while Putz had retired from everyday labor two years prior.)

"None of your business, nosey," he retorted, closing the L.L. Bean catalog and tossing it upside down on the stack next to him. "Why don't you pull up a chair and stay a while? As if I had any choice in the matter."

"Hey, why so feisty this morning? Mrs. P not make your eggs right?"

"I make my own eggs and you know it. Want some coffee?"

"Sure."

"If you must know," he said when he returned with a steaming cup, "I am trying to replace my old white hat, but I am not finding it an easy task, because I do not want the same style. I feel I need a new image."

I was surprised at how fast he explained his dilemma.

"You must have been dwelling on this for some time," I said.

"Oh, I have. I have tried on all kinds of toppers in stores. Nothing has said 'Yes! This is it!' to me. Maybe I'll find something at The Mall of America."

"*You* are going to the mall?" I was taken back.

"Yeah, well, we are going to stop by there on our way to K.C.

this trip. Just a slight detour. Mrs. P, bless her heart, wants to stop and see our godson and his family, and they live near the mall, so...you know."

And so they went to "The Mall."

And here is how P tells, in his own words, two weeks after their return, when once again we were sharing a cup, how he found his new hat.

"We got to the mall about 1:30 in the afternoon, and took a slow tour of maybe a quarter of the area in three hours. It's not that bad, I guess. It is a big place. Some of the stores run vertical instead of horizontal. A bit weird. Anyway, I made two purchases. One, a special little Beanie Baby, for myself, and *my new hat!*

"You bought a Beanie Baby?"

"And my new hat! Like it?" He interrupted his tale, producing the replacement "icon."

"See, it is wide-brimmed, has a leather chin strap, so it doesn't blow off my head, AND, I can snap up one side of the brim, Aussie style. When the love of my life said I looked like Hemingway, that sold me, right then and there.

"But I played the sale cool. I didn't grab it right on the spot. I waited. I put it on again...tilted it...snapped it up...let it down. Then put it back on the rack.

"We were finishing our tour, when I went back to the hat place. I found the proper size, and, again, I put it on straight, cocked it, snapped up the side. The clerk thought it looked so good on me she reduced the price a bit...and I only mentioned a senior citizen discount three times."

"Very nice," I said. "Now, what's with the Beanie Baby?"

"Oh, that. Well, you know how I like to hunt those little Timberdoodles. Well, they just happen to have a Woodcock Beanie Baby. I just couldn't resist. It's called 'Beak.' Someone said it was some other kind of bird. A kiwi, I think, but it is a woodcock to me. Not often one gets to set a 'doodle' on his computer. How do you really like the hat?"

"It's fine. Not really you, though. 'Course you did say something about changing your image. It's fine."

And so P decorated the hat with all his pins and faithfully wore it everywhere for about a month. Then one day I ran into him on the street.

"Do you realize the comments going around about you and that hat?" I asked.

"I do. But that is a part of wearing a hat with character," he replied shifting the fedora on his head. "Selecting a hat should be more than just being practical, it should involve some vanity and ego," he added as he continued on his way.

So, Putz had a new hat.

What about the old one? Did he dump it?

Of course not.

The old white hat, blotches and all, has been semi-retired to the truck—ready and willing, when needed. This change created another move. The old "truck hat" has become the "garage hat" at the cottage, in Wishigan Country. (Some things will never die, if Putz has anything to say about it.)

The "new" hat now is decorated with an antique fly, two pins, and a few feathers. It sits on its special "rack," the head of a stuffed beaver toy, and awaits P's bidding.

It is now only worn for special occasions.

Putzer replaced "the Hemingway look" before anyone but Mrs. P realized he had it. He ordered a new spring, summer, autumn everyday hat from the catalog two weeks after he got back from the trip. A green, fully brimmed, floppy soft, fly/trout-decorated hat almost exactly like the white one he semi-retired. (Guess he really didn't need that new image after all.)

Does Putz have other hats?

Of course. Each one has character and reflects the required image Putzer wants to emit for the occasion:

There is the new everyday spring, summer, fall hat, just purchased, and, of course, the "new, special occasion Hemingway hat."

There is the everyday winter hat, a full-brimmed tweed.

A fly fishing hat, long brimmed with ear and neck protection from the sun.

There are three Kromers, those well known caps, in a variety of colors—one for skiing, one for hunting, and one for "just because."

And finally, there is the long, blaze orange stocking cap that is only used with the blackpowder guns.

Some folk, not to mention any names, just like to confuse others by changing their image every now and then. (Or so he thinks.)

Until we meet in, on, or near the river,

Keep a good thought!

The Peshtigo Putzer

Biking the Bearskin

Once again the Ps go to their bikes to enjoy the outdoors. This time they head into the Minocqua area of Wisconsin. They discover trout streams, and swim with loons. All because of a bike hike.

They awake to the same sounds that serenaded them to sleep last night—the haunting laugh of the loon—a sound long associated with wilderness areas. They, however, are not exactly in the wilderness. They are camping at Indian Mound State Park, on Lake Tomahawk, in the Northern Highland/ American Legion State Forest, between the towns of Lake Tomahawk and Minocqua. Pretty...semi-remote...but not wilderness.

Putzer, in one of his more introspective moods, says to his wife, buried in her cocoon-like sleeping bag next to him, "It just goes to show, God's feathered and furred creatures adapt quicker to change than man does. And we are supposed to have all the smarts. Huh!"

"What's that supposed to mean?" comes a muffled reply from somewhere in the cocoon.

"If you don't understand the connection with loons, wilderness, and man, it is too early in the day to try to explain it. Come on, it's time to rise and shine."

It's early September, and the morning has just the proper touch of autumn to it. The Putzers scramble from their snug sleeping bags, and hustle into warm clothes—long pants, t-shirts and sweatshirts are in order this morning—it may be only shorts and t-shirts later in the day, but not now.

A few yards from shore two loons, the objects of earlier conversation, a mother and her offspring, are looking for breakfast. (Mr. and Mrs. P could distinguish the mother from the young by the difference in coloration—the youngster did not have the distinct black and white markings; it was quite grey. Their size, however, was almost identical.)

Mother does most of the diving, but as time goes on, after offering her youngster a small minnow to show it what is on the menu, the adolescent must also dive for its meal—there is no free lunch, even in loonland.

They dive and surface and feed for about twenty minutes in front of the campsite. The Putzers watch the entire teaching process while sipping the first cup of hot tea and/or coffee. What fun.

After having their own breakfast—coffee, juice and a hearty bowl of oatmeal with brown sugar—the Ps load their bikes on the back of the truck and head for the reason they came to this part of the state, Minocqua and the Bearskin Trail. (The name alone is intriguing.)

Putz hasn't a clue where the trailhead is, so he stops at the local Trek bike shop to ask. (Hey, guys do ask for directions—sometimes!)

"A block down to the stop and go lights, a right on Front Street, two blocks to the Post Office and a right into the parking lot behind the Post Office," directed the young man in the shop.

And so it was.

When they arrived, the parking lot was full of blue t-shirt clad senior citizens holding their own "Olympics."

Putzer wondered if they would be interrupting the athletes, or if they could even get to the trail.

"Don't worry," one of the participants said. "We're finished. The trail was never a part of the event anyway. It's all yours!"

The Putzers load up the bike bags with lunch, water, cameras and binoculars. (They are now in shorts with the layered t-shirt/sweatshirt combination.)

The trail is 18.2 miles long, one way. Their goal for the day is to ride the north half, a total of eighteen miles back and forth, and do the south half tomorrow. The Putzers bike like they ski or walk or snowshoe or canoe, or most any activity they participate in, taking their time to enjoy a trail and its amenities. It is what they do best. To just bike a trail to say they have done so is never in their game plan.

The trail begins with the crossing of a portion of Minocqua Lake, on the first of many wooden trestles they will peddle over before the day is done.

The path is primarily crushed, rotten granite—well-compacted and mostly smooth riding.

They pass several back yards of private residences, some resorts, and a business or two, but mostly they are in the woods—pine and oak and maple and birch and aspen. The trail borders lakes and small ponds, streams and creeks with tag alder, and tamarack/berry/sedge marshes and bogs. The smell of the pines is wonderfully pungent and overwhelming. Picnic tables are scattered conveniently along the entire trail.

At the halfway point the Putzers shed their sweatshirts, and take advantage of the restrooms, drinking water, and tables with a view of South Blue Lake.

"What a beautiful rest stop," says Mrs. P as they sit at one of the tables, taking a little break.

"You feel like turning around and heading back?" asks P. "This is halfway, but it's still early. Want to continue?"

"Sure. Let's go ahead and when I think it's far enough, I'll let you know," replies Mrs. P.

"Let's go!"

As they peddle further south, the landscape changes to creeks and springs with trout and chubs and all the beautiful wetlands that go with them, dominated by the trail's namesake, Bearskin Creek.

Oh, there are others too—Rocky Run, Scott Springs, Horsehead, and Harshaw. Each crossing is marked and trestled in wood, and each bridge has a sign that denotes its length and its number, i.e.: 425, G-37; 425 feet long and trestle number 37.

Like most trails they have been on, this one has mile posts telling how far the Putzers have gone from where they started. Also, every road crossing is named along with the distance to the trailhead they were peddling toward.

The trail is wonderfully maintained, and because it is an old railway bed, all but two of the grades are naturally slight. The two "high hills" are in the south half. They are blacktopped to prevent erosion.

As they approached the "big hills," a diversion from the original trail, Putzer hits some soft gravel and almost takes a spill.

"That was close," Mrs. P says. "Just what we would need, three-quarters of the way through the trail and you go wiping out on me. Don't do that!"

"Like I planned it," Putz mumbles to himself.

They stop at an observation deck overlooking one of the larger wetland areas. The walk from the trail to the deck crosses Bearskin Creek. In the creek are trout and chubs, feeding.

The trail is full of sights and sounds. There are asters and bergamot and even some white water-lilies blooming. Chipmunks, their antenna tails in the air, and gophers, keeping their tails low to the ground, scurry across the trail continuously. Squirrels, grey, red, and even black, cross their path. Bluejays and robins and chickadees and little brown warblers with yellow rumps flit, and an eagle soars. A doe perks her ears and stares as she hesitates before disappearing into the tag alder.

They stop at another small tumbling creek. As they watch the water, an elk bugles.

"What was that?" asks Mrs. P.

"A bull elk," replies Putz.

"How do you know what an elk sounds like? You've never been west."

"I've heard and seen them on hunting shows on TV. Trust me, it's an elk. There he is, on the other side of the fence, on that ridge. See him? Oops! He's gone."

Ducks quack and gabble, and sandhill cranes rattle their eerie cry.

They have a perfect day for biking. However, as Putz points out, "A few weeks from now, these tamaracks will be dressed in burnished gold. Combine that color with the color of the pines, and we could, temporarily, rename the trail, "The Packer Passage," because we would be traveling in a world of green (pine) and gold (tamarack).

As they peddle, Putz makes a mental note, (which he later writes down because...well you know) that if they ever return in summer, he will pack his fly rod and only do the south half. He will take all day and try his luck in the miles of brooks and creeks that hold trout.

If you haven't already gathered, they did bike the entire trail, all 36-plus miles, with ease, having enough time for a swim in the gin-clear water right at their tent's back door, cooling their bodies wonderfully. (How about that, they begin in sweats and end in swimsuits. Who could ask for more?)

They topped the swim off with a couple of cold ones while preparing a meal of Noodles Alfredo, green beans, and sliced ham fried in butter and brown sugar. All on the good old Coleman two-burner.

A campfire and loon music again ended the night as the sun set and the chill of autumn settled on the woods.

Soon they were once again tucked into the sleeping bags, drifting around in dreamland.

Until we meet in, on, or near the river,

Keep a good thought!

The Peshtigo Putzer

Saving Money on Fly Tying Material

It may sound like only fly fishermen would be interested in this tale, but don't be misled. Hunters can use this advice to help their friends, and there is a definite connection for you ladies too.

Ever wonder what a fly fisherman like Putzer does in the fall of the year? I mean, now, during late September, October, and November, fly fishing in Wishigan Country is quickly coming to an end.

The trout season on the inland streams will cease. The optimum time to fling feathered frauds for the warm water species is gone. Oh, there are still steelhead and salmon runs going on in the Oconto, lower Peshtigo and Menominee, but let's face it, unless you live near these rivers, fly fishing is a dead issue.

The season is over.

It is time to wipe down the rods and check the windings, clean up the reels, store the lines, order new leaders, and settle in at the ol' fly-tying bench and spend the winter tying—replenishing your supply of frauds for next year.

That is what Putz does, right?

Wrong!

Let me tell you, any fly fisherman who ties his own flies, as Putz does, and is worth the price of the tackle he totes, is out there right now sweating his buns off trying to refurbish his cache of tying supplies. (Fly-tying material doesn't grow on trees, you know. Critters? Yes. Trees? No.)

How does Putz gather some of his tying material, you ask? What rigors of discomfort and long hours does he put himself through in order to refill his supply of natural tying materials?

Allow me to elaborate.

This time of the year, autumn, Putzer is out there trudging through the tall timber; pushing and pulling his "pirogue" into the cattails and muck of the marshes; and hiking the long hot fields of stubble and corn; straining the sinew of his legs and fibers in his feet to the max; collecting fur and hair, feathers, and tails.

Yes, and he's doing it in the name of *economy*. He knows he must be *frugal*. (Which, in his case, is not a problem. He has actually been called "cheap" by the other member of the family.)

Putz knows it doesn't take long to ring up a bill of $50 to $100 for fly-tying material. However, P has learned over the years that, with proper planning, he can save a goodly portion of that bill by going out and collecting his own. So, like the pioneers of old, he becomes a true hunter/gatherer.

Don't laugh! Pay attention and learn. (And you ladies out there might want to read this too, so you will understand.)

How does Putz begin this process?

He lays out a very concise, detailed route that takes him to places where he is at least 51 percent certain of success in the collection process. With a map in front of him, he researches the websites for the most recent updates of current conditions and game populations.

This year, he will begin the excursion with a trip to northwest Wisconsin to secure grouse and woodcock feathers. (Grouse feathers make magnificent tails and fins on a Woolhead Sculpin, and the miniature woodcock feathers make wonderful wings.)

A few days at a resort his wife and her girlfriends use each spring, with both excellent food and maid service, in the heart of Grouseland ought to get that done. Especially, if he can hit the Timberdoodle flight just right. And, if the hunting gods smile on him, he might even be able to take a short break from all that work and relax a bit and try to pick up a musky—maybe. Sort of a self-reward for all his efforts.

From there he will swing south and a bit farther west to the

Mississippi, where P will collect a few mallards and wood ducks. (His supply of mallard breast feathers for Hornbergs is really low.) His chances will be best there, and he can help fill the home freezer with walleye filets during the midday slow hunting hours. It will put a lot of pressure on his time, but he will do it to help with the family food budget.

On his way back to his home in southeastern Wisconsin, P will pass through the Driftless Area. Here he will pause a day or two to chase turkeys around and over the hills and farm fields in this beautiful southwestern part of our state. This effort should get him the feathers he needs for Muddlers.

Now let's see, from there P will make a small jog into the central part of the state for squirrels. He has a friend who has a cabin there, where he can bed down for a night or two. The oaks in that part of the state are full of grey and fox squirrels. (Their tails make the best streamers.)

Then, if he could not find one along "Ol' Man River," Putz

will swing down into one of the private blinds around the edges of the Horicon National Wildlife Refuge, so he can harvest some goose wings. (The perfect grey for a lead wing Coachman, and of course, there is no substitute for good fresh goose biots for the tail, legs, and antennae of stoneflies.)

He'll pick up a red squirrel when he goes deer hunting for a week or two in November—need that hollow deer hair for bass bugs, and the tan and white tails for more streamers. Nothing like combining trips to save money—a little here, a little there, it all adds up.

Now what's left? Oh, of course, pheasants. (He needs those golden tippets for the tails of the Royal Coachman and Pass Lake, and the tail feathers for nymphs.)

Well, pheasants are pretty hard to come by without a dog, which Putz does not own, so he best go to one of the local game farms and arrange a hunt with one of their pointers. Yes, that would be smart. No sense traveling all the way to the Dakotas when you can do it locally. *Economize, that's the name of the game.*

Putz will pick up the rabbit and fox fur after the New Year, when the weather has had a chance to get cold, and they develop thicker coats. If he's lucky he might even be able to call in a coyote. (He understands that the new electronic calls work well. Might not hurt to look into one.)

Now, is there anything else? Some gamecock hackle, but a trip to Africa is out of the question. He would never go without Mrs. P, and the price for two might tip the scale of economy too far to the wrong side. Yeah, he'll have to buy that from a catalog along with peacock herl, hooks, floss, thread, foam and the other synthetics.

Well, he can't collect everything he needs. Some things just have to be bought.

All in all it seems to be a good plan. Probably cut his bill at least in half, maybe even seventy-five per cent. Plus, he should be able to add some meat to the larder.

Of course, this does put a few extra miles on his truck, so he may need to look into a new one before next year. But, he'll need one sooner or later anyway. Besides, they are offering zero per cent right now, so that will also save money.

But won't Mrs. P be proud—saving all that money.

You know it's just like when **she** comes home from a day at the mall and says, *"Honey, you won't believe all the money I saved you today. Come help me unload the van."*

Until we meet in, on, or near the river,

Keep a good thought!

The Peshtigo Putzer 

A Foray into Kansas

The Putzers never thought they would be traveling in Kansas. How many people do? But then, one of their daughters moved to Kansas City, Kansas. 'Nuff said.

"Why do you want to travel in Kansas? What *is* there to see?" asked the Ps at-the-time-but-not-now son-in-law. "The only way to see Kansas is to head west from here on I-70, put the pedal to the metal, and watch out for the tumbleweeds. When you get to Colorado…you've seen Kansas."

"Really? Not according to my research," replied Putzer. "I see things like rock formations, historical forts and towns, and according to your local *Nature Conservancy* office, there are some great birding places, which should have local nesters and some new early-arrival migrants this time of the year. That's enough of a reason for us. We certainly won't see everything, but I figure we can get an overview of the landscape, and add a few birds we'll never see in Wisconsin to our species list."

And so it was, on a Monday in September, that the Putzers left Kansas City on a four or five day, "quick trip, viewing Kansas."

They did use I-70 as their main artery, but mostly they drifted north and south from it, mainly south, using it only when practical. They did come close to Colorado, but it was not their goal, so they never crossed the border.

Their first stop was Kanopolis State Park—Kansas' oldest state park. They had a variety of campsites available, from primitive tent areas to accommodations for RVs and motorhomes. The park offered fishing, swimming, boating, and trails for hiking, biking, and equestrian accommodations.

The Ps selected a pad in the Eagle Point area—near the water, with shade. Shade was rare…and a definite advantage on a day like this. (It was 90-plus, sunny, and humid.)

The site consisted of crushed rock with a picnic table, fire pit, and electricity. The shore of the reservoir, and the beach, was only forty to fifty yards away.

After they set up camp, Mrs. P slipped into her swim suit, picked up one of their aluminum lawn chairs, and literally sat in the lake. Although the water had a cooling effect, she received the full blast of the sun.

P opted instead, at least for the time being, for the shade and moving air, hoping that the heat would moderate when the sun went down.

After supper that evening, Putz put on an old pair of tennis shoes, broke out his fly rod and waded the beach area, catching a white bass or six. Mrs. P watched from her chair.

They found lots of wildlife: turkeys, turkey vultures, prairie dogs, deer, geese, ducks, great blue herons, gulls, terns, cormorants, kestrels, bluejays, bluebirds, flickers, and warblers.

When they moved on in the morning, an island was covered with white pelicans.

The next day they decided to take a quick look at some rock formations before going birding at Cheyenne Bottoms and Quivira National Wildlife Refuge.

In a light rain, the Ps took a close look at Mushroom Rock, with its many "inscriptions"—both ancient and modern. Then they headed west to find Pyramid Rocks. They found that the road leading to them was closed for repairs.

So, they backtracked. They traveled state highways and local roads to Castle Rock. Castle Rock stands, very lonesome-like, in the middle of a field. The sun was preparing to set when they arrived.

It was dark when they pulled into Cedar Bluff State Park. The wind was howling and it was starting to rain. After a quick light supper, in the front seat of the truck because of the rain, they retreated into the back of the truck.

Thunder and lightning gave them a show. Eventually, the rain slowed to only an occasional drop or two.

About two a.m. Mrs. P nudged Putz awake and asked, "What is that smell? I think it's smoke." (She was still lying down.)

P sat up and looked out the rear window of the truck. "It's smoke alright." he said calmly. "We have a grass fire on the hill behind us."

The fire was about a half mile away. Cars were moving up and down the park road.

Mrs. P asked, "Now what?"

"Well, first we put our clothes on so we are ready to move, if necessary."

As they were changing from night clothes into day clothes, fire trucks appeared on the scene, and the rain began to intensify. Between the firefighters and the deluge provided by God, or Mother Nature, the fire died. The Putzers eventually went back to sleep, but didn't change out of their day clothes.

After a well-needed breakfast of pork chops and eggs and toast, they headed for the showers.

Have you ever shared a shower with tumbleweeds? They did. The showers had no roofs. The walls were concrete block, but there were no roofs. Tumbleweeds, and a few crawling critters, were in every corner. The Ps took quick showers.

The forecast was for more rain and colder weather. The Ps didn't mind colder, but clouds and rain were not conducive to good birding or photos.

They headed east for Quivira and Cheyenne Bottoms, but detoured slightly to have a look at Fort Hays.

Located on the southwest corner of the city of Hays, they learned, among other historical facts, that this was actually the second Fort Hays built—the first one was destroyed in a flash flood in 1867.

From here they passed through Post Rock Country. Miles and miles of fences with posts made from stone cut from the bedrock that resides near the surface of the earth. When quarried, it is soft and can be cut and shaped with a hand saw. Later, as the air "cures" it, it becomes "hard as a rock"—pun intended. Because of the ease with which the rock can be cut when freshly unearthed, it is called Greenhorn Stone. The foundations and the entire blockhouse at Fort Hays were built from Greenhorn.

The Ps arrived at Quivira National Wildlife Refuge ten minutes before the office closed for the day. The attendants gave them a self-guided car tour folder of the refuge. Fortunately, as they took the tour, they had a peek or two of sun. They left two and a half hours later. Again the clouds had taken over and it was almost dark.

The self-guided auto tour took them to salt marshes, grasslands, small impoundments, some cropland, and a few small wood lots.

The Ps hiked a few of the short trails that led to water, and with the aid of binoculars and spotting scope, they added several new species to their bird list—snowy and cattle egrets, glossy ibis, black-necked stilts and lesser yellow legs. In addition, they enjoyed seeing the more familiar birds: great blue heron, common egret, mallard, teal, marsh hawk, and coot by the thousands. Again, they saw white pelicans.

Their original intention was to do Quivira and Cheyenne Bottoms in the same day because of their proximity to each other, but they ran out of time on Wednesday, so they did Cheyenne on Thursday.

"Cheyenne Bottoms is a complex of marshy basins in a 41,000 acre lowland area containing the largest system of wetlands in Kansas. The water is centered in a natural basin-like feature fringed on three sides by limestone, sandstone, and shale bluffs." So says the Welcome brochure produced by The Nature Conservancy, Kansas Chapter.

Between the lands owned and operated by the Conservancy and the State of Kansas, birders and hunters share the sights and sounds of migrating shorebirds and waterfowl during the fall migration season. Only non-hunters get to enjoy the spring migrants during March and April. (Not surprising, the groups are mostly one-in-the-same.)

The Ps found two auto tours available. One, on Kansas State property, rides the dikes surrounding Pool Number One, while the Conservancy Trail gives you a trek through their lands to the northwest. While the state trail is generally drivable, the TNC trail handout cautions, "After heavy rains the roads through the Conservancy's property are impassable."

The Ps roamed the dikes in an on-and-off rain. It had been raining on and off for two days, and because this was all new territory for them, the Ps did not explore the Conservancy Trail. They saw many of the shore birds of yesterday and a multitude more of ducks.

They left the Bottoms in a drizzle, which followed them to Milford Lake, then continued during a quick view of Konza

Prairie. They had hoped to see bison at Konza. (They did a few years later, actually walking among them, but that is another story.)

With more rain scheduled for tomorrow, the Ps decided to cut the trip short, and headed back "home" to K.C.

"Well, did you see enough of Kansas?" asked their K.C. family.

"Well, we scratched the surface," replied P.

"We found that Kansas is a whole lot more than just freeway and tumbleweeds," added Mrs. P.

Until we meet in, on, or near the river,
Keep a good thought!

The Peshtigo Putzer

'Twas the Night Before the Muzzleloading Season

We end this collection of tales with one told in a different style of narrative. It is a story that can happen anywhere, but not to everyone. Only a deeply dedicated putzer.

Twas the night before the muzzleloader season, and spread on the cabin floor,
Were trappings, and gear, and paraphernalia, galore.

And there, in the middle of that mighty pile,
Stands a man—bearded...pudgy...with a grin like a child.
He speaks not a word, but goes straight to his task,
Checks off each item, as he sips from his glass.

His long johns are a combination of both new and old.
Polypropylene for the sweat, wool for the cold.

Next in the pile is a turtleneck sweater.
(To keep the wind from his neck, there is nothing better.
It may be black or dark green or maybe navy blue,
Very little of it shows—any color will do.)

There hangs the wool shirt—
Plaid, without a doubt!

Socks?
Poly and wool—can't go without.

The pants too, originate from sheep...maybe, a blend.
They keep you warm, even if you get wet in the end.

The boots are Pacs—rubber bottoms, leather tops.
Insulated and oversized so circulation never stops.
Not even after sitting an hour or three,
When your only movement is brought on out of necessity.

The old mackinaw hangs on the back of the chair,
Along with an insulated liner, for when the air
Gets nippy and damp, the kind that chills to the bone,
(Without the combination, it could send you home.)

A vest of blaze orange, and a stocking cap with tassel, too.
It's the law, 50% from the waist up, so other hunters won't shoot you.

A red sash 'round your waist adds a nice traditional touch.
(It's one you won't see in the woods very much.)
If made correctly, it will hold knife and drag rope.
(You could add a .50 caliber pistol, if you wanted to cope,
With those you would meet along the way,
And were able to ignore the things they might say.)

The powder horn will hang from one shoulder,
And cross to the opposite side.
As does your Possibles Bag,
Made from deer hide.

Inside the bag the items needed are arranged, organized, and neat:
Speed loaders, caps, nipple pick, quick starter, ball puller, and something to eat.

Everything, it appears, is ready
For tomorrow's day of fun!

Oh, no!...My God!...I don't believe it!
He forgot to bring his gun.

Until we meet in, on, or near the river,
Keep a good thought!

The Peshtigo Putzer

Author's note: The photo was taken at a time when Putzer did not forget his gun. I use this to emphasize that Putzer does, on occasion, like to portray an image when he does things. As referred to in the tale, "Of Hats And Images, It's Tough To Change."

Epilogue

A final word or six.

First and foremost, I thank all of the parties involved in the creation of this book. (They are listed elsewhere, so there is no need to name them again.) It took me three years before I could make it a priority. After that, it went relatively fast—another year and a half. I will tell you this, it was quite a learning experience, being my first book, and almost self-published (a story in itself).

The design of this book went through many changes. The decision to repeat the ending after each tale was batted about often. I have kept it there, because this is not a book designed to be read completely through in one sitting, as with a novel. This is a book to be read a chapter or two at a time. Consequently, the ending is a part of each story, so it stayed.

The mixing of photos and sketches was also a dilemma. To the best of my knowledge, most books of this genre do either one or the other, not a combination. The fact remains that the column, in which many of these stories first appeared, does use both. Therefore, so does the book. Let's face it, sometimes a drawing just works better than a photo, but not always.

The question "Who is Putzer?" can never be answered totally. Putzer is sometimes a real person, sometimes a composite of people and or events. I will tell you this: all of the stories are true. The adventures, or misadventures, if you prefer, all did happen. Not one story is pure fiction.

Have some of the tales been embellished? It is called *poetic license*. Poetic license is, and has been, used ever since the first story in time was repeated, whether by the printed word or verbally or through some form of art.

Does that mean that all the humor is poetic license? Definitely not! Putzer lives with mishaps. It is his expected way of life, and not only in the outdoors. If you don't believe me, ask Mrs. P. (Who is also very real.) Besides, the truth is funnier than fiction. Always has been, always will be.

Is this the end of the Putzer columns, now that there is a book? I certainly hope not. I intend to keep his "tales" in front of the public as long as I can find a publisher to print my trivel. (My word, "trivel." Gordon MacQuarrie used *drivel* so well, I hesitate to use it, out of respect for him.)

j. k.